PRIZE SURPRISE SWEEPSTAKES!

This month's prize:

A FABULOUS SHARP VIEWCAM!

This month, as a special surprise, we're giving away a Sharp ViewCam**, the big-screen camcorder that has revolutionized home videos!

This is the camcorder everyone's talking about! Sharp's new ViewCam has a big 3" full-color viewing screen with 180° swivel action that lets you control everything you record—and watch it at the same time! Features include a remote control (so you can get into the picture yourself), 8 power zoom, full-range auto focus, battery pack, recharger and more!

The next page contains two Entry Coupons (as does every book you received this shipment). Complete and return *all* the entry coupons; **the more times you enter, the better your chances of winning!**

Then keep your fingers crossed, because you'll find out by November 15, 1995 if you're the winner!

Remember: The more times you enter, the better your chances of winning!*

*NO PURCHASE OR OBLIGATION TO CONTINUE BEING A SUBSCRIBER NECESSARY TO ENTER. SEE THE BACK PAGE FOR ALTERNATE MEANS OF ENTRY, AND RULES.

**THE PROPRIETORS OF THE TRADEMARK ARE NOT ASSOCIATED WITH THIS PROMOTION.

PRIZE SURPRISE
SWEEPSTAKES

OFFICIAL ENTRY COUPON

This entry must be received by: OCTOBER 30, 1995
This month's winner will be notified by: NOVEMBER 15, 1995

YES, I want to win the Sharp ViewCam! Please enter me in the drawing and let me know if I've won!

Name_____

Address _____ Apt. _____

City   State/Prov.   Zip/Postal Code
Account #_____

Return entry with invoice in reply envelope.

© 1995 HARLEQUIN ENTERPRISES LTD.   CVC KAL

PRIZE SURPRISE
SWEEPSTAKES

OFFICIAL ENTRY COUPON

This entry must be received by: OCTOBER 30, 1995
This month's winner will be notified by: NOVEMBER 15, 1995

YES, I want to win the Sharp ViewCam! Please enter me in the drawing and let me know if I've won!

Name_____

Address _____ Apt. _____

City   State/Prov.   Zip/Postal Code
Account #_____

Return entry with invoice in reply envelope.

© 1995 HARLEQUIN ENTERPRISES LTD.   CVC KAL

"Are you going to try and keep avoiding this forever, Ruth?"

"I'm not trying to avoid anything," she insisted. "I didn't ask you to come. I didn't ask you to...to..."

"To try and save my marriage—*our* marriage—while there's still time?" Kurtis replied.

"It's over."

"It is not over." And now his eyes fairly blazed. "It's not over until we *make* it be over, and that, dear lady, we have yet to do."

Victoria Gordon is a former journalist who began writing romances in 1979. Canadian born, she moved to Australia in the early seventies and now lives in Northern Tasmania. She has judged retrieving trials for gundogs and is active in a variety of other outdoor activities when not chained to her magic word-processing machine.

A Magical
Affair
Victoria Gordon

Harlequin Books

TORONTO • NEW YORK • LONDON
AMSTERDAM • PARIS • SYDNEY • HAMBURG
STOCKHOLM • ATHENS • TOKYO • MILAN
MADRID • WARSAW • BUDAPEST • AUCKLAND

There *is* a Ruth who *is* a witch, and this must be for her.

ISBN 0-373-17251-6

A MAGICAL AFFAIR

First North American Publication 1995.

Copyright © 1994 by Victoria Gordon.

CHAPTER ONE

RUTH didn't remember noticing the envelope when she'd grabbed up her mail in the final, splashing run to the relative sanctuary of her doorway. Not surprising, she now thought, considering the flood of rain across her glasses, the driving torrent that had sluiced her wavy dark hair down across the nape of her nurse's cloak.

And yet...she *should* have noticed, even then. Snug in her rocking-chair, the soothing flicker of her fireplace slowly massaging warmth into her exhausted body, she could only stare at the unopened missive and wonder at the apprehension it caused.

No return address—hardly significant. She didn't recognise the typeface in which her Launceston address was typed. There was nothing, really, all that unusual about the envelope. So why the *frisson* of sensation that crept light-footed along her spine?

'I'm getting spooked,' she murmured aloud, then shivered visibly as she mentally scolded herself for doing so, hearing *his* voice in her mind, laughing, telling her she only talked to herself so she'd be sure of liking the answers. But she denied him now, thinking, It's probably the music, accepting and yet denying that there, too, he remained a part of her.

Scarcely heard in the background was the almost sole legacy of Ruth's short-lived marriage; the love of baroque music created in her by Kurtis Goodwin tied him to her in memory, but the soothing magic she found in

5

it was of itself sufficient to outweigh his influence, sometimes enough that she could almost forget him.

She closed her eyes for a moment, revelling in the warmth, the quiet of the soothing music, then turned her attention again to the envelope and its invisible aura of disquiet.

She reached out, withdrew, then reached again with one close-cropped fingernail, tentatively inserting it beneath the envelope's flap. A quick, decisive rip and it was done; but Ruth still had to force herself to free the heavyweight bond—only a single sheet, she noticed—from its containment.

As she huddled in the chair, it seemed that the entire room had taken on an aura, threatening, unseen, but somehow tangible, striding over the music with a dominating tread that reminded her of Kurtis's forceful movements.

Shaking her head, flinging that memory away, she took a deep breath and flipped the single sheet of paper open, only to fling it away from her and lurch to her feet with a cry of soul-wrenching pain as she read the salutation.

'Dear my lady witch', it said; and her suddenly drunken brain took in only those four words as the paper fluttered towards the fire, Ruth almost following in her panic.

She had the presence of mind to clutch at the letter, snatching it from the flames despite all of her *being* crying out to her to leave it; let it burn. But even once she'd saved the letter, Ruth found it impossible to force her vision past that salutation and the haunted visions it dragged from within her.

Shaking her head violently, she strode into the hallway to stand, all—one hundred and fifty-six centimeters—

five feet one and a half—trembling as she stared at the stranger's face in her mirror.

Witch? Easy to believe now, she thought. Her hair, ever unruly in its tortured waves and now roughly towelled dry, floated round her head in a dishevelled ebony halo. Her large, pale grey eyes—eyes she'd been told so often could change at will from serenity blue to fury green—were just grey now. Pale grey, death-grey, a colour she had seen all too often as a skin colour in the nursing home where she now worked. And huge! They seemed to dominate her face, the pupils thrust into black relief against the lightness of her irises.

She looked away, then back, seeing no change and expecting none. The lips of the image trembled, drawn back into a fearful smile that revealed slightly pro-tuberant canine teeth that for all of her adult life she had felt marred her smile, making it a thing seldom freely given, and always self-consciously. Schoolmates had ridiculed them; even her mother had once remarked upon them unkindly. Ruth had never quite forgotten that comment, coming as it did after the dentist had declared it too late to alter the situation without drastic measures at an unaffordable price.

Only Kurtis had—at least in the beginning—seemed immune to such comment. 'They're part of you,' he had said, dismissing her flawed image as irrelevant in the face of his love for her... 'For all of you. As you are; as you will be.'

Ruth stared into the mirror, wallowing for a moment in this image of her uglier than he'd *ever* seen, then flung herself away, rejecting the impulse to self-pity.

'Who ever heard of a witch without a gap tooth' she growled as she hunched in her rocking-chair, eyes captivated by the dancing flames and arms wrapped round the pain inside her. Pain helped not at all by repeating *his* words out loud.

Eleven months, she thought. Eleven months since she'd fled the emptiness of their hollow, impossible marriage. Another month and she would have been free, delivered from the shame and failure by the twelve-month separation rule of the Family Law Court.

Eleven months. Longer apart than married, she thought, and sneered, because they'd been longer apart even *while* married, if the truth be known. Looked at from the distance granted by time, she wondered if they'd ever been together at all.

'Dear my lady witch'... Ruth cowered in the chair, unable to bring her tear-misted eyes past those four words. She felt herself twitching like a dog in the fire's warmth, her nerves so jangled she could hardly hold on to the single, terrifying slip of paper. Her eyes slid out of focus, making the dancing flames a featureless curtain beyond which lay memories...

She had met him first at a party given by a fellow nurse, when she was living and working in Hobart. To this day, she didn't know what fickle threads of fate had brought either of them to the party; she herself had decided to go only at the last possible instant. She wasn't a party person. She liked her crowds small and manageable or big enough to hide in. Non-threatening. This party had been anything but, and she'd sought solace from the thumping music and seemingly inane activities by tucking herself in a nook between wall and refrigerator in the darkened kitchen alcove, wine glass in hand and mind in neutral.

She had been on her third glass, past her usual limit, when Kurtis Goodwin had stepped into the room carrying with him that aura of command she now always associated with him.

He, too, had had glass in hand, but he had paused in the act of opening the fridge door to peer down at her, his eyes obviously still adjusting to the alcove's low lighting. The silence between them had stretched until Ruth thought it would snap like a weakened elastic before Kurtis had spoken to her. His voice was rough, like tyres on gravel. Rough, low, yet somehow alive with a strange power. And an accent... not Australian, she'd thought; North American?

'And what are *you*?' he asked, teeth bared in a wry, subversive grin. 'Not a dishwasher, surely?'

Ruth blamed it on that third glass. Surely there was no logic to the way she revealed her own teeth in a savage smile and croaked as best she could manage.

'I'm the kitchen witch,' she replied. 'Show respect, sir, or I shall turn your wine into water.' The she lapsed into silence as she saw laughter rising in his eyes like a flood. It was no mirage; she saw it, recognised it, and for some strange reason relished it.

He couldn't have been much above average height, she realised, but in the closeness of the situation he fairly loomed above her slight, diminutive self. Dark, perhaps slightly auburn hair with flashes of grey above his ears. Eyes... some colour, but too dark here to be revealed. And it wouldn't be their colour that first registered anyway, she realised, but their weariness, their expression of world-worn sadness.

Late thirties? Early forties? Impossible to tell with a man like this. Those wondrously compassionate eyes seemed a hundred years old; the rest of him denied it. He was poised before her like an athlete, had moved so when he entered the room.

He stayed unmoving, silent. His eyes roamed almost carelessly along the length of her, and Ruth sensed he was quite literally memorising her. She could feel those eyes, weary, tired, but *knowing*, almost tactically touching her at points throughout their journey. Her response was involuntary but none the less severe; her nipples throbbed to that tangible caress, her tummy went all fluttery and she had the most insane urge to thrust out one shapely—or so she'd been told—leg in a model's pose to assist his assessment.

'Not much of you,' he finally commented, returning his eyes to meet her gaze. 'But then I suppose that isn't important, if you really *are* a witch.'

'I'm very large in spirit,' she quipped, astonishing herself in the process. What on earth was she doing? Ruth had never considered herself excessively shy—reserved was perhaps a better description—but neither was she usually this flippant.

'Oh, I can see that by the way you're getting into that evil red,' he grinned. 'Seeing I have control of the fridge door, I'd be happy to fill your glass if you'd be so kind as to empty it.'

'Not a chance,' Ruth replied without thinking. 'I'm the original two-pot screamer, and this is my third.'

'Ominous,' he replied. 'Haven't you got some spell or another to counter the effects?'

'The best of all,' Ruth heard herself saying. 'It's called abstinence.'

And to her astonishment he laughed, a genuine, lusty, honest laugh, followed by a shake of his head before he turned those incredible eyes upon her once again.

'I've heard of virgin queens, but a virgin witch is well and truly beyond my experience,' he chuckled. 'Probably not surprising since you're my first witch of any kind.'

'That *wasn't* what I was talking about,' Ruth snapped before she had time to think, then could have kicked herself—or him! He'd deliberately led her into that, and his eyes fairly shouted his triumph at succeeding.

'Good.' Just the single word, but it spoke volumes, accompanied by the look in his eye. Suddenly her safe little niche between fridge and wall made her claustrophobic. She could feel her breath shortening, her body tightening in a poise for flight. But flee where? This suddenly dangerous stranger blocked her only exit, unless she truly *could* fly.

And, as if he'd read her mind, the man shifted his body so as to block her exit less, to give her room to move if she really wanted to. Not without having to press past him, touching him, increasing her awareness of him—one didn't need to be a witch to realise that. But still there was a certain courtesy in the gesture, as if he had sensed the threat and deliberately removed it.

'I don't suppose,' he suddenly said, 'that, being a witch and all, you might have a decent spell to counter three days without sleep? I'm so overtired I think I've forgotten *how* to sleep.'

'You'd hardly need a spell, then,' she replied, her training rushing to the fore as she suddenly realised the man before her was swaying on his feet with exhaustion. 'All you need to do, I expect, is lie down somewhere.'

And she stiffened, waiting for the obvious 'your place or mine' response, suddenly aware of just how stupid she might be being. But he fooled her, and Ruth found great satisfaction in that, somehow.

'Social obligations prohibit it,' was the reply. 'I'm here more on business than for pleasure, and from the looks of it I'll be toughing it out for a few hours yet.'

'Well, then all I can suggest is that you give the grog a miss,' she found herself opining. 'Otherwise you're liable to need a wake-up spell, not a sleeping pill.'

'I seldom drink,' he replied, making the statement neither a brag nor an apology. 'Do witches have names, by the way? Mine's Kurtis Goodwin.'

'Ruth Chapman,' she replied, and found herself dipping a slight curtsy in response to his slightly wavery bow. And he was smiling. Even half dead with exhaustion, he exhibited a quirky sense of humour she couldn't help but like.

So when he reached out for her hand, she accepted the gesture, only to catch her breath with complete astonishment as he slowly, deliberately, lifted it to meet his descending lips, never taking his eyes from her own.

Insane, she whispered in her mind. Yet couldn't help but be drawn by the intensity of the moment. This man might be playing games, but his eyes said he took even his games very seriously. His lips touched her hand in a genuine caress, and his eyes fairly glowed as they poured seduction into the entire gesture.

When he murmured, 'My lady witch,' Ruth caught her breath once more, astonished at her own reaction. For just an instant she felt as if her sedate little black dress had been transformed into a dazzling evening gown, as if her rowdy hair had suddenly become tame and managed, as if the dingy little kitchen alcove had become a medieval room, a magic place.

Just for a moment, but it startled her. And this must have shown, because he released her fingertips even as she flinched inwardly at the strangeness of her feelings.

'Every second woman in the place tonight seems to be a nurse of some kind,' he said then. 'Are you...?'

'At Calvary,' she replied. 'And you?'

'I'm what used to be known as an entrepreneur before the label became something of a dirty word,' he replied with an enigmatic grin. 'Speaking of which, I'd best return to the fray before my business interest falls in love or some such thing and the whole performance goes down the tube.'

He shook his head, the gesture as weary as his eyes. 'This has been a helluva trip,' he muttered, speaking as much to himself as to her. 'I love Hobart, but sometimes I wonder about the way they do things here.'

'You'd do better to go home to bed,' Ruth said impulsively. 'I don't see how anybody could concentrate on business in the shape you're in.'

Which gained her a sudden, rueful grin.

'I've been doing it for twenty years,' he said. 'And while my shape mightn't be as...bewitching as yours, don't go writing me off as a geriatric yet. I've got plenty of good years left.'

'I wasn't...' She paused as his eyes told her he hadn't been at all insulted by her earlier remark, was merely stirring a bit.

'Of course you weren't. A proper witch—and I'm dead certain you are a *proper* witch—would have used her second sight to see me as I really am,' he said. 'But, on the other hand, a proper witch could probably cast some sort of spell on this bloke I'm dickering with so that he'd be as tired as I am; then he could stop trying so damned hard to impress me with all the gorgeous girls he knows and I could flee back to the Sheraton and my lonely but oh, so welcoming bed.'

The Sheraton... 'You're not local, then?' A silly thing to ask, she told herself even as the words emerged. Of course he wasn't local; everything about him fairly shouted at a worldliness far beyond Hobart's parochial confines. Not that it was anything specific—his suit displayed careful tailoring, the gleaming shoes looked expensive, and the thin gold watch she'd seen revealed as he'd taken her hand also fitted the mould of wealthy, worldly businessman.

But who could tell, these days? So much of everyone seemed to be a façade, and in business suits all men looked much of a muchness. Except, she realised, this one. His persona was too strong, too thoroughly defined, to be of any but his own making.

'Not local anywhere any more,' he replied. 'Canada, originally, mostly Australia these days. I had a home once, but I sort of lost it in the wheeling and dealing, to be honest. Just now I'm basing myself in Sydney, with clothing stashes in half a dozen other big cities.'

'You don't sound as if you like it much,' Ruth said. 'Why do you do it if you get no pleasure from it?'

'All I know how to do, and when it's good it's very, very good,' he replied, again with that wry, cynical grin. 'Like the little girl with the little curl——' and his hand lifted to touch at Ruth's rowdy locks '—right in the middle of her forehead.'

'When she was good she was very, very good and when she was bad she was horrid'. The words of the nursery rhyme tripped through her mind, but Ruth was far more aware of the light gentleness of his touch, the way he made a simple gesture into an intimacy.

And then, too soon, he was turning away to rinse his glass at the sink, fill it with water, and down the contents in a gesture both weary and savage.

'Right,' he said, quite obviously speaking to himself. 'Up and at 'em, boyo!' He moved towards the doorway, then paused, spun on his heel, and bowed low towards where Ruth still stood.

'My apologies, lady witch,' he murmured with a half-grin. 'But do I have your permission to withdraw? Less pleasant than our dalliance, certainly, but business does await.'

Ruth's hand extended itself as if with its own life, and as he bent his lips to it with a secret smile she heard herself speaking flowery words of permission while the touch of his mouth against her fingers sent tendrils of... something that rippled through her entire body. Something quite inexplicable, but very, very nice.

She stayed for a moment, in awe of both the situation and her reactions to it, then followed Kurtis Goodwin out into the pandemonium.

He didn't stay long after that. Ruth noticed him deep in conversation with another man in business clothes, then with their hostess. And twice she caught him looking at *her*, his sad eyes gentle with some unspoken message, one cocked eyebrow acknowledging her existence, but he didn't return to her and when she looked a few minutes later he was gone.

Gone without so much as a farewell... It bothered her for some obscure reason; she found herself thinking of him, seeing those eyes in her mind as she drove home not much later. Sliding into sleep, she felt again the touch of his lips on her fingers, even more so that curiously intimate touch at her forehead.

'You've made an impression, whoever you are,' she murmured drowsily, enjoying the reflection. But it was morning before—driven awake by a rap on the door instead of the expected birdsong—she began to see just how impressive Kurtis Goodwin could *really* be!

The bouquet of flowers was gigantic, sufficiently overwhelming that Ruth was almost able to ignore the fact she was accepting them—dressed in a hastily donned housecoat—from a cab driver who kept grinning at some joke she felt must be on *her*.

But it was the note that knocked her flat. The note, or just the incredible weirdness of the whole situation.

'Dear Ruth the witch,' it began, in handwriting so bold as to be almost overpowering. The note apologised if it had arrived too early, suggested witches should not need vast amounts of sleep anyway, then went on to thank her for her consideration of the previous evening, commented on their 'delightful conversation'. It went on to plead with her to join the humble writer in 'a late breakfast, perchance?' with an added flowery request for her to then show 'your humble servant' the quietest part of Hobart she knew, and was signed with a signature only his banker could recognise, though Ruth had no trouble.

All of it, needless to say—and not one bit surprising, for some reason—in the most flowery language possible. Like something from a medieval play, considerably overdone.

It was the little addition below the signature, however, that had her reaching for the telephone book to find the number of the Sheraton and accept before she lost her very nerve.

'Warlock, apprentice grade', he'd written, adding one of those inane, decorative parcel stickers—this one of a little horned gremlin with a ladybug on his nose.

Ruth was still chuckling when the telephone rang in his room and she heard that gravelly voice, surprisingly free of tiredness, answer.

'The quietest place I know might involve a bit of a walk,' she said, not bothering to identify herself, certain somehow that he would know, would expect this call to be her.

'I need a new pair of boots anyway,' was the calm reply. 'Presuming, of course, you mean what I expect you do. Meet you in the lobby in fifteen minutes?'

'Half an hour,' she found herself replying. 'I have a...a cauldron on the boil.'

'Just go easy on the eye of newt, then,' came the rasping reply. And he was gone, leaving her with a humming line and a strange feeling of well-being that bordered upon pure elation.

Ruth dressed hurriedly in jeans and trainers and a warm sweatshirt, gave her hair a cursory brushing that changed virtually nothing, and was parked outside the Sheraton well within time. But when it came to actually walking into the building, she found herself suddenly strangely shy.

All very well to play games, she found herself thinking, but I'm out of my league here. This is risky stuff! And knew, somehow, that risky was a fair description despite the apparent safety of breakfast at nine on a fine Hobart Saturday.

This with a man who could manage in the dead hours after midnight to find a totally appropriate parcel sticker, organise flowers, and have all delivered to an address he could only have gained, she realised, from their hostess of the evening before. Kurtis Goodwin had left the party without a farewell, but he'd certainly not forgotten.

Her curiosity won. Whatever else, Kurtis Goodwin was the most unusual male animal she'd met in recent memory; the first, indeed, to make her laugh in a very long time.

'Ensorcell him, witch,' she muttered to herself as she squared her shoulders and marched determinedly up the steps. 'He's sort of handsome and maybe he's rich; maybe he'll take you away from all of this, show you how the other half lives.'

She entered the lobby to find the warlock, 'apprentice grade', now comfortably dressed in much the same style as herself, and with a welcome in those world-weary eyes that turned her trepidation into a puff of smoke.

His courtly bow over her hand, the briefest touch of his lips to her fingers, drew a few raised eyebrows from among the morning crowd in the lobby, but Ruth scarcely noticed. She was caught in the trance he created with his eyes, which she now noticed, irrelevantly, were a sort of greeny blue with hazel flecks.

Thankfully, he kept the performance to a minimum over breakfast, a meal that Ruth felt certain would keep her going for that day and the next. Essentially a vegetarian herself, a hangover from student days when meat was too expensive a luxury to the point where she'd actually lost the taste for it, she had no compunction about watching her host get round a healthy breakfast including the traditional steak and chops and eggs. Her brief, practised explanation for her own taste drew only a quick grin and a cheeky reply.

'Rabbit food,' he said, then added, 'But look what *they* get up to.' And, although certain she didn't blush, Ruth felt as if she had.

He accepted her assurances, over coffee, that he really wouldn't need boots for the easy bush walk she had in mind from The Springs to New Town Falls.

'Just remember you're dealing with a suspected geriatric here,' he scoffed. 'I may have to be taken by the hand if I can't make the grade.'

'It's only about a twenty-minute walk and there's hardly any grade——' she started to assure him, only to halt at the gleam in his eye, the curiously triumphant expression.

'But maybe I'll just *want* to be taken by the hand,' he interrupted, reaching out to take her wrist in his fingers, holding her still with his eyes as he did so.

Ruth sat transfixed by the intimacy of the gesture, then got all flustered by the intensity of his gaze and ended up neither saying anything nor pulling her hand away.

It wasn't until Kurtis himself, once again as if reading her mind, released her that Ruth realised how utterly pleasant the sensation of his touch had been.

'You'll give yourself indigestion if you keep that up,' she countered, finally. And forced herself to meet his eyes. Not easy; the hazel tones kept flickering, their depths filled with some message she felt sure she ought to understand but didn't. A dangerous message, no doubt, for this man already seemed so complex, so contradictory that he simply couldn't be safe.

Not, certainly, when he countered with comments like,
'I rather expect you'd have some sort of spell against
that thing, provided I asked nicely enough.'

'No spells in daylight,' she replied lightly, not meaning
it and knowing that he knew it too. He just grinned that
quirky grin, his eyes drinking her in.

He kept almost entirely silent as they drove up Davey
Street, following the road that then turned to creep along
the shoulders of Mount Wellington. But his eyes were
on her as much as the scenery, and she was ever aware
of that. Ruth at first found herself chattering like a de-
mented tour guide, but eventually Kurtis's silence began
to affect her, and she stopped. Which for some strange
reason felt better, felt right, as if they didn't need mean-
ingless words between them.

He insisted she pull over into the first significant
lookout point, and she sat and watched him as he walked,
panther-smooth, to the edge of the overlook, then stood
like a rock to stare out over the sea and the various distant
headlands. Hands on hips, hard-muscled legs tight
against the fabric of his jeans, he appeared to her as
solid as the mountain itself, though she found it a strange
impression to consider.

They parked at The Springs, then walked the pinnacle
road to where the Lenah Valley track began. The Lenah
Valley track—complete with signpost clearly stating
walking time each way to New Town Falls.

Ruth read the sign, certain in her soul she'd never seen
it before, then glanced at her companion in the futile
hope that he might not have noticed. He had; she was
certain of it. But not a single word or gesture, not even
so much as a raised eyebrow, betrayed him.

Then the moment was past and they were starting down the gentle slope of the track itself, and it was too late for Ruth to speak. Not least because the track was so narrow, it forced them into single file, and of course Kurtis let Ruth take the lead. He did so with a broad, expansive and courtly gesture, but the unholy glint in his eyes made it only too clear he was starting to enjoy her discomfort.

She stepped out strongly, wishing she could regain control of the situation, wishing indeed that she could admit she hadn't been on this track for half a dozen years, and that she hadn't *meant* to mislead him about the timing... Wishing even more that she'd worn looser jeans; she could feel his eyes with her every stride, and began to hope he'd stumble or something, just to get his mind on his own walking, not hers.

She stepped up the pace until they reached the first place where the forest thinned to reveal views of Hobart, then halted to exclaim in her tour guide's voice, 'There— isn't that beautiful?'

'Indeed,' he replied with a nod. But his eyes were on her face, not on the countryside that rolled away below them into the southern suburbs. His eyes roamed across her features as easily as their feet had trod the well-made track, and again Ruth had the sensation that he was memorising her, taking her every individual feature and storing it somewhere inside his head.

It was a strange feeling, not tangibly unpleasant, yet mildly discomforting. There was an intensity there, almost an intimacy. Had he made to touch her, even to take her hand, Ruth felt she would have fled. But he didn't, and the feeling left her when she started moving again.

They paused only briefly at Junction Cabin, then headed down into the steepest part of the walk along a fire trail, now walking side by side but, for the most part, in silence. The setting almost demanded silence; their path was flanked by enormous trees, great stringy-barks and blue-gums that seemed to have erupted from the barren mud-stone soil.

At their own level, the various native bushes thrust their spiky way through the ubiquitous ferns, some abundant with bright red flowers. Once, Ruth would have remembered all their names, but suddenly her memory had deserted her. It was, she thought, as well Kurtis didn't ask any pertinent questions, or she'd have been mightily embarrassed.

But he stayed silent, and, when they turned into a narrow trail leading to the falls, always behind her. She didn't have to listen for his step, didn't have to look around. She could *feel* his presence, *feel* his eyes. Once again she found herself over-aware of her long walking stride, of the sway of her narrow hips, and knew that awareness was only making it worse. Dared she turn around quickly, she thought, it would be to find him laughing at her discomfort.

When they did finally reach the falls, Ruth heaved a mighty sigh of relief. Memory, she was certain, had betrayed her; it just *couldn't* have taken this long the last time, she thought—and, having lost her concentration, slipped on the greasy rock where the track slithered across between the upper and lower falls, and would have fallen but for Kurtis's hand on her arm.

'Easy,' he murmured, and it was the tone of someone settling a fractious horse, Ruth thought. Nor did he release her arm, but stood there, looking up at the top falls with its masses of rock and fallen timber, seeing the view with his eyes and seeing Ruth with his fingertips.

No part of his touch could have been termed cheeky or crude—he merely maintained his grip on her forearm—and yet his touch, the sensation of him, seemed to inundate her entire body.

When, after an aeon's silence, he gently turned her to face him, when fingers like thistledown lifted her chin so that he could stare silently into her eyes as he lowered his mouth to hers, Ruth was powerless to resist even if she'd wanted to. And she didn't do either.

His kiss was gentle, searching, tender. His lips felt right, tasted right. And while he kissed her his fingers brushed at her cheek, wandered the column of her neck in a gesture both caressing and reassuring. Melting, she felt as if her bones had dissolved to jelly, *had* to hang on to him, *had* to let her hands know the security of his shoulders, then the touch of *his* neck, the feel of the crisp hair at his nape.

All in stillness but for the plunging water, the never-silent quiet of the forest around them, all somehow connected with the magic of that place, the rightness of the situation.

Not until he had released her mouth, not until he had physically let go of her, stepping back to put some actual distance between them, did either of them speak.

'That,' Kurtis said, 'was indeed magic, my lady witch.' And he grinned, a genuine, warm, if rather quirky grin that turned her tension to mist, then shredded it and blew it away with the breeze.

Ruth could only nod agreement; it had indeed been magic, but she was damned if she'd let him realise just *how* magical for her. She didn't dare! No sane person could feel such emotion with someone still a stranger, she thought—only to realise he wasn't a stranger, hadn't been a stranger since they'd shared a few minutes of intimacy in someone else's kitchen. That he would never again be a stranger, perhaps, because he had touched something in her, something basic.

It was too intimate, she thought, too intimate and too tempting. Which was probably why she made a hurried attempt at conversation without thinking it out first.

'I'll bet you didn't know this stream runs fair in front of my unit,' she said. 'And I actually think it's bigger here than it is there, although of course it couldn't be, could it?'

'Logic says not,' he replied, 'but streams do funny things; maybe it goes underground or something.'

'It has trout in it...where I am, I mean.' She blurted the words, now suddenly edging into a form of panic because she knew he was going to kiss her again and knew she wanted him to kiss her but somehow, at the same time, didn't want him to, lest it spoil the perfection of that first kiss.

And as if sensing her concern, he turned away to walk ankle-deep into the pool at the base of the top fall, kneeling to scoop up water in his cupped hands and drink.

'Want some?'

'Not enough to do *that*,' Ruth replied. 'That water's too cold for me.'

'Come this way,' he said, pointing to a series of stones which would bring her almost to him, but dry shod.

Ruth did so, only to find that the curious intimacy of trying to drink from his hands made it practically impossible. She managed a few sips, then overbalanced and ended up as deep in the pool as he, joining in his delighted laughter at her mishap.

'Now we can both walk ourselves dry,' he said with a grin. 'It won't be as bad as you think, and at least now I can be assured witches can't walk on water, which is nice to know.'

Ruth didn't quite share his enthusiasm for starting the trek back with soaking feet, but the alternative—staying any longer in this magic place with this curious man— had unknown dangers she preferred not to risk.

And somehow when they made the long walk back the trail had become wider, because there were long stretches where space existed for Kurtis to take her hand and walk beside her, and he did. And she wanted him to.

When they reached Junction Cabin, he tugged at her fingers until she paused, then turned her into his arms for another kiss, this one delivered with the same silence, the same deliberate slowness as the first. The message was clear, unmistakable. She had time to resist, time to withdraw from his embrace, if she wanted to. She didn't.

Nor did she when they paused—and kissed—at the tiny Rock Cabin, and again at the junction with the track to Sphinx Rock Lookout. But she could have! His intentions were clear—could hardly have been clearer!— but everything in his demeanour seemed geared to ensuring her freedom of choice.

The final bit of the track up to the road forced them once again into single file, so conversation continued to be non-existent until they had actually reached the bitumen, whereupon Kurtis made a great show of looking at his watch, the time-direction signs for the walks, and his watch again.

'Well, Ruth the witch,' he finally said with a shake of his head, 'you may be wonderful on spells and potions, but your sense of timing leaves a great deal to be desired.'

Ruth, who had consulted her own watch surreptitiously and who, too, had realised they'd taken almost exactly two hours each way, slower even than the signs had suggested, much less her 'brief walk' definition, had no excuse and she knew it, but she had, at least, to try.

'Time is irrelevant to a witch,' she declared haughtily, posing, shoulders back, one arm extended to the sky. 'After all, when you're eternal...'

'And when you're a witch, you can make time stand still anyway,' he replied with a hint of a grin. 'I grant you that, my lady witch, most willingly.'

But then he dropped the performance and slid precipitously into a seriousness that struck Ruth like a blow to the stomach.

'You have a rare and amazing quality of serenity about you, Ruth,' he said. 'I felt it when we first met last night; it was like a great wave of calm that fairly washed me off my feet.'

'Piffle, sir. You were merely overwhelmed by my witchly charms,' she replied in a frantic bid to defuse the intensity in his attitude. 'Warlocks—and especially mere apprentice-grade types—always do. It is,' she sighed, 'one of my fatal charms. And besides, you were asleep on your feet in the first place. You shouldn't have been partying; you should have been in bed.'

'Last night—true,' he admitted. 'But how do you explain today? I'm wide awake, I had a short but reasonably good sleep, and the whole time I've been with you has been a sort of slow, gentle, placid dream. I haven't felt so relaxed in years, and I mean that.'

Damn it! she wanted to cry. Don't do this to me. Because she had felt much the same, but lacked the words, the confidence, certainly, to say so. Being with Kurtis had involved a magic quality that made her claims to witchbreed dangerously blasphemous.

'All part of the service,' she finally replied, still desperately seeking to soften the intensity of his gaze, of his words. 'We take our tourism responsibilities seriously here in Tasmania.'

And she saw, actually *saw* the glow fade from his eyes, almost felt him shake his head as if to force a return to the here and now from wherever his intensity had taken him.

They drove in an almost liquid silence up to the pinnacle of Mount Wellington, where icy winds quickly forestalled any major wanderings, at least on Ruth's part. Kurtis, seemingly immune to the biting chill, slid into his warlock role long enough to beg her witchly permission, then disappeared for nearly half an hour among the masses of jumbled boulders on the mountain's barren crest.

On his return, he flashed her an enigmatic smile, but— somewhat disappointingly—offered no kiss. And he was strangely quiet, she thought, on their return journey to the city.

It wasn't until they were nearly downtown that he asked if she had further plans for the day, suggesting if she didn't he would be delighted to continue sharing it with her. So they went to the museum, then wandered through the craft shops and gift shops in Salamanca Place until dinnertime, discussing anything and everything and nothing in particular.

And throughout Ruth kept noticing how she actually could *see* the marks of tension and strain washing from Kurtis's face as if being dissolved by successive ocean waves. By the time they paused for dinner at the Ball and Chain Grill, he was visibly tired, but so relaxed he appeared not to notice.

'Is there any known way to trap a witch and keep her?' he asked in the relative seclusion of their restaurant booth. 'You're good for me, my dear lady; I'm not sure I'm going to be able to do without you, now that I've been touched by your spell.' And his fingers reached out to take her wrist across the table, then began to stroke tantalisingly at her pulse, which immediately quickened to his touch.

Too fast, too fast, screamed her mind, but her body, her very being, screamed just as loudly about how very *good* being with him was.

'Or is it like trying to capture a unicorn?' he added while her confused mind hogtied her tongue. 'I don't know where I would find a virgin in this mortal world, but I suppose if there is one Hobart would be the place to look.'

Ruth raised one eyebrow, suddenly cautious, but he merely grinned and continued.

'Well, as the song says, I've been everywhere, and Hobart's the first place I ever found a witch. Loosen up, Ruth the witch. What's the sense of making all this magic if you're not going to enjoy it?'

Loosen up? Easy for him to say; it wasn't *his* heart that kept leaping to keep pace with his touch, with the warmth in those sad, sad eyes. It wasn't *his* body that was being systematically sensitised to the touch of a virtual stranger who somehow was no stranger at all. It wasn't *him* who was confused, damn it!

'You'd be smarter to go after the unicorn,' she finally managed to say, only to have *him* raise an eyebrow.

'Evasive,' he replied. Too perceptive by half.

'I . . . I don't know what else to say,' she replied. 'I don't know exactly what it is that you're asking.'

His fingers continued their enchanting journey along her wrist, his eyes probed her gaze, straying occasionally to meander across her face, down to the hollow of her throat.

'I'm saying, my dear lady witch, that I like you very much and that I'd like to see you again,' he answered. 'I don't know how you do it, but the effect you have on me is quite something else again. But if I'm going to see you again, it might be nice to know if you *want* me to do so.'

'Well, it's your choice, surely,' she replied, confused now, uncertain. Of course she wanted to see him again, but surely that was obvious?

Then the obvious struck her like a hammer-blow.

'You're married?'

His gust of laughter was explosive. 'No,' he said. 'Dear witch, I'm as free as your gigantic spirit.' And then, his eyes reflecting his seriousness, 'But I was married; she died last year. Does that make a difference?'

'No,' Ruth said, more confused than ever now, and furious with herself for having created most of it. 'It just seemed sort of an obvious question, that's all.'

'Well, if it matters, it was probably the worst marriage ever endured by any two people on this earth,' he said then, and his eyes blazed with that frightening intensity.

'Was it your fault?' Ruth asked the question because it seemed, to her, the obvious one. Only after the words were out did she realise how terribly personal a question it might seem. She had already forgotten they'd only met less than a day ago.

His shrug and lifted eyebrow confirmed his words. 'Most of it, I suspect. A fair half, anyway. No matter what people say, it usually works out that way if you're fair.'

'I'm...sorry,' Ruth said. Because she was. Her own parents, now both dead, had lived a marriage of pure hell while it lasted, and gone on hating each other to the end.

'So am I.' That simple, direct statement ended that part of the discussion. Kurtis signalled for the bill and within minutes they were walking hand in hand along the Hobart waterfront to where Ruth's car was parked near the Sheraton.

When they reached it, Kurtis dismissed the vehicle with a minute shake of his head and a subtle pressure on Ruth's fingers. They kept walking, and with every step she grew more apprehensive. Did he, she wondered but didn't dare to ask, hardly dared even to think of it, expect her to go with him to his room? It wasn't the idea that spooked her so much as the feeling that she wanted to, might even do so. Madness, this.

But he didn't, didn't even glance at the imposing structure as they walked past the front of it. And they carried on, hand in hand and in silence, along that block, and the next, and the next, wandering aimlessly through the quiet evening streets, peering into shop windows, occasionally looking at each other, but saying nothing.

Occasionally they met and passed similar couples, usually obvious tourists, usually elderly, and to each Kurtis offered a nodded acknowledgement, occasionally a low-voiced, 'Good Evening.' But to Ruth he said nothing, except through his touch. And it seemed to her that when one of those elderly couples revealed, as some did, the visible evidence of two people truly comfortable with each other, still in love at an age many never attained, his touch altered subtly, his grip on her fingers just that hint tighter.

She accepted it, enjoyed it, was thrilled and entranced and frightened by it. Everything about Kurtis seemed such a strange combination of gentleness and rightness and that vivid, deep intenseness.

And all too soon, it seemed, they were back at her car, although how they got there she couldn't remember. She had no memory of having steered their route, couldn't imagine how he could have done it.

'I don't want this to end; I think you know that,' he said, now holding both her hands in his and staring down into her eyes. 'But I have to catch the red-eye in the morning, and I really ought to have *some* sleep. And I'm sure you could do with some; it's been a rather long day for you.'

'I'm not on duty until Monday,' she replied, meeting his gaze, almost trembling with feelings she couldn't understand and didn't dare to question.

'I shall write to you, my lady witch,' he said then, 'if you want me to.'

'I'd...like that, I think,' Ruth said.

'Even if it's a love letter?' And the teasing in the question held a curious ring of truth. 'Because I might, you know. I fancy I've been quite ensorcelled by you, whether you actually cast the spell or not.'

'It would be far, far worse if I had,' she replied brightly, trying to defuse his intensity, trying to still her own leaping emotions. 'You'll get over it in time, sir warlock. I promise you.'

'Promise me you'll answer my letters instead,' he countered.

'No promises,' she whispered, but too late. His mouth swooped down to claim her lips and this time there was a thirst in his kiss, a thirst that drank from her lips, a hunger that she could feel in his body as he pulled her close and held her there.

Her breasts were crushed against him, her thighs against his so that she couldn't help but feel his passion. His fingers orchestrated a magical tune along her spine and his breath was as sweet in her mouth as the wild berries she'd had for dessert.

But then he stopped, lingering as he drew away from her, but clearly determined. Because Ruth was no longer in control, and perhaps they both knew it.

'This isn't the time or the place,' he said. 'And the only other places I can think of, while highly tempting, wouldn't be right.'

And even before Ruth could think, he was kissing her hand in that mock-courtly fashion, and murmuring, 'So goodnight, my lady witch, but not goodbye!'

And he was opening her car door, handing her into the vehicle with a gallant bow, closing the door behind her. And he was gone, walking away without a backward glance and without a single word of farewell from her.

Not even the chance to say thank you for the breakfast, the dinner, the most incredible day of her life. Leaving her, she decided as she drove slowly homewards, both speechless and entranced. Just as he'd intended!

CHAPTER TWO

'DEAR my lady witch...' Staring into the ever-swirling, ever-changing flames, Ruth fingered this latest letter, this totally unwanted, unexpected letter, breathing slowly and deeply as she summoned up the courage to read it.

Again, she managed only the salutation, although her peripheral vision picked up the occasional following word despite her unwillingness to read further. Then she folded it again, quickly, her fingers flying in a frantic, fevered haste. She laid it on the side-table while she went and made a cup of tea, wishing for the first time ever in her life that she smoked, just so as to have another excuse for delaying the inevitable.

It would be, she knew, a masterpiece of its kind. *His* kind. Kurtis had always been fastidious in his letters despite their frivolous nature.

Frivolous! She almost laughed at the thought. His letters might have been couched in the most flowery of language, had certainly made extravagant use of witches and warlocks and medieval poetry, but they were anything but frivolous.

From the very first, he had laid bare his deepest feelings, his most intimate thoughts, the intensity of his very self. Or so it seemed. It had been a masterpiece of seduction by mail, and should that ever be declared a crime—as it ought—she would be happy to testify against him and happier still to watch him hang!

'Dear my lady witch...' His first letter had begun so. She had received it on a Tuesday, plucking it eagerly from the mailbox in a flurry of disbelief and anticipation.

He *had* written; despite her wanting it so very much, Ruth truly hadn't expected ever to hear from Kurtis Goodwin again, and just the sight of his handwriting on the envelope had given her goose-bumps.

And the letter inside had been everything she could have hoped for and more. Couched in the language of a warlock of lesser standing than she in her witch role, he had used guile and mock-humility and the wackiest sense of humour she'd ever encountered to report on his flight to Sydney and then to Brisbane and then to, of all places, Darwin, from where the letter had come.

'Dear my lady, it would be assumed the modern craft of flight would be at least more comfortable than a broomstick,' one line began, 'but be assured, your radiance, that it is not so...'

The rest, covering several pages in that flamboyant, bold handwriting, became a hilarious tale of an epic journey, then subtly shifted gears to become an intimate, probing examination of a relationship in the making, and it was haunting, filled with promises of wonder.

The letter which arrived three days later was even more surprising. Written in expectably flowery language, it was none the less a masterpiece of intrigue and devilry, clearly designed to appeal to her sense of curiosity and certain of success. It contained a clipping about a forthcoming Sydney stage production—one which would never be staged in Hobart—and a most curious invitation.

Dear my lady witch...

Please note the attached advertisement and take suitable cognisance of this once-only, never-to-be-repeated, genuine, you-beaut, shouldn't-be-missed offer!

You consult your crystal ball and or frogs' entrails or whatever to pick the date you might like to flex off for a day or two or three to hie yourself northward for a visit, and I shall provide:

Transport as required.

Bed and board—yes, I *can* cook; even rabbit food

Dinner and drinks and the theatre

Scintillating—if perhaps geriatric—companionship throughout.

Dress: optional—although probably necessary for dinner and the theatre

Intentions: Mine—strictly honourable unless persuaded otherwise. Yours—persuasive? Please consult crystal ball.

The letter went on to include a telephone number for the expected RSVP, then Kurtis's flamboyant signature as warlock, apprentice grade, and a postscript:

One hopes you're at least tempted by this splendid offer—thus: 'The only way to get rid of a temptation is to yield to it.' Oscar Wilde: *Picture of Dorian Gray*

Ruth read it, shook her head in wonderment, read it again. She took it with her to work—she was on afternoon shift—and found time to read it a dozen times before she got home again.

And with each reading the preposterousness of it all became greater and her instinctive caution became less as curiosity—as he'd known it would!—took control.

But, most of all, every time she read the letter—she laughed!

Nobody ever, she thought, could have received such a weird, totally inane invitation. And she laughed again, revelling in the insanity of it all.

She read it again immediately on getting home, then picked up the telephone with her laughter ringing through the flat and dialled his number while she still had the nerve.

'Sir warlock, you are mad, mad, mad,' she laughed when his familiar, grating voice answered.

'Does that mean yes or no?' he replied without hesitation. 'I presume, of course, that it means yes; otherwise you wouldn't have phoned.'

'Methinks you presume a great deal,' she replied cheekily, smiling to herself in surprise at just how *good* it was to hear his voice, rich with feeling.

'Methinks I must, my lady witch,' was the chuckled reply. 'But you can scarce blame a poor, apprentice-grade warlock for the results of your own witchcraft.'

'I'd only be able to come for the weekend,' she said, serious now as if in protection from his jesting, flamboyant tone. A tone, Ruth thought, that could end up bewitching *her* if she weren't careful.

'I don't care if it's only for the night of the play,' he replied, suddenly serious himself. 'It may be the only time I'll be able to see you for quite a while, and——'

'But it's ridiculously expensive, even for the whole weekend,' Ruth interrupted. 'Are you sure you've...thought this out?'

'As sure as I'm talking to you now,' he rasped, voice now, amazingly, alive with an emotion Ruth couldn't quite identify. 'And you let *me* worry about the expense, if you don't mind.'

'I'd have to,' she replied. 'If it were up to me, I couldn't afford to make it to the theatre *here*, never mind in Sydney——' And then she broke off, awkwardly, realising how that might sound.

Kurtis ignored it, obviously already ahead of her in his thinking.

'And may I presume you've decided on *which* weekend?' he urged. 'It would be nice for me to know, so that I can start organising.'

'Oh, the thirteenth, of course,' Ruth replied. She'd determined that almost before deciding to accept in the first place. It was a Friday, that month, which somehow seemed auspicious even if she wasn't certain why.

'I wonder why I'm not surprised?' was the reply, accompanied by a chuckle at Ruth's gasp of obvious surprise at the comment. 'Right, Friday the thirteenth it is, then. Any particular flight you'd prefer...considering I presume you'll have to wait until after work?'

'Oh, evening, definitely,' she said. 'I won't be off until about four, so I suppose it will have to be after six if I'm to have time to change and get to the airport and all.'

'As good as done, my lady witch. The tickets will be in your hand within the week.' And in the background she could hear a telephone's insistent pealing.

'My other phone is calling,' Kurtis said, distraction obvious in his voice. 'I'll try to call you back if I can, but things are pretty damned hectic here just now, so you may have to wait for a letter instead.'

'That's all right.'

'Have to be, won't it? Give my love to your "familiar" and tell it I wish it were me.' And he was gone with no other farewell, no sign of...of what? she wondered. What did she expect—a declaration of undying love?

That she didn't get during the three weeks of waiting for the auspicious date heralding her trip to Sydney. Nor did he telephone again. What Ruth did get, however, was nearly everything else and nearly as good.

Letters! Letters almost every day, it seemed, and each one containing in its flowery, formal language another tiny nugget revealing some infinitesimal aspect of the man behind them. For Ruth it was like trying to put together a jigsaw puzzle without ever seeing a picture of the finished item. Kurtis was so complex a person, so rational-irrational, logical-illogical, she sometimes found his letters almost incomprehensible.

In one, he mentioned a book of poetry he'd bought at some obscure second-hand book shop. *Forty Singing Seamen and Other Poems* by Alfred Noyes.

Published in 1908, given to somebody for Christmas—according to the flyleaf—in 1914. And—can you imagine it, my lady witch?—nearly half the pages uncut! All these years squatting on some bookshelf, somewhere, and never even read. It's enough to make you weep, is it not? Such a fate for a book of poetry, to languish unread for almost eighty years. Of course somebody's read *The Highwayman* or at least freed the pages *it* was on. But to read that utterly wondrous saga of love and death and passion, yet never even bother to read the rest of the book...barbaric, my lady, truly barbaric! I shall attempt to make amends

by reading it aloud to you, as poetry ought be read—
by candlelight, with wine and soft music.

Barbaric! And, she thought, to Kurtis it would be
exactly that. He lived with words, loved words. He
should have been a writer, perhaps *was* in his own
peculiar way. Certainly his letters were like nothing she'd
ever encountered.

She smiled to herself, then frowned at the next
thought, which considered his involvement with words
as an entrepreneur, which even she knew was a twenty-
dollar word for huckster, at least according to some
people.

Many people. The thought had her wondering how
much she really knew about the man. Entrepreneur, she
knew, might cover a multitude of sins and probably did.
He had never told her much about his work, only that
it involved vast amounts of travel, a good deal of buying
and selling and wheeling and dealing.

The thoughts crept ghost-like along her spine, but Ruth
shrugged them away almost angrily. This is silly, she
thought; all he's done is invite me for a weekend of
theatre and... Now her thoughts crept along different
parts of her, touching her breast, moving in small ripples
through her tummy and lower to leave her squirming in
her chair.

And...what? For the first time the 'what' took on
the meaning she realised it should have from the start.
Was this to be a so-called 'wicked weekend'? And, if so,
was she ready for it?

Pondering on the issue accomplished less than nothing.
All it did was increase the momentum of the emotional

pendulum Ruth was clinging to, making things worse instead of better.

But Kurtis, as if he'd been reading her mind—and doing it better than Ruth herself—resolved the issue as much as it could be resolved in the letter which arrived the next day.

'The guest bedroom will undoubtedly welcome the company,' he said. 'I've been trying to remember when it was last called into service and can't; you may be the first overnight guest I've ever had sleeping there.'

Which, Ruth determined, could mean everything or nothing. Which was probably his intention. She shook her mane of unruly hair and grimaced. How uncharitable. All he'd done was try to make her feel more comfortable, to ease a concern she recognised herself!

'And all you can worry about is what overnight guests he's had sleeping with *him*,' she muttered, and sneered at herself, fangs bared, in the mirror.

Her biggest problem was in answering his letters. She had none of his facility with words, felt genuinely in awe, sometimes, of how much he could say both on the lines and between them. And too often she wondered if what she read between the lines was what Kurtis intended or what her increasingly facile imagination *wanted* to find there.

So Ruth kept her own replies light, breezy and—she was sure—so bereft of her true feelings that he would never guess how much more nervous she became about the whole trip with every passing day. Nor that the days without a letter had become worse than the days when she received one.

Until suddenly time seemed to telescope. One day the trip was a lifetime away, the next it was Friday the thirteenth and she was flustered and flighty at work and then rushing home to change and waiting nervously for the cab to take her to the airport.

Then she was in an aeroplane for the first time in her life, leaving Tasmania for the first time in her life, and the minutes stretched into weeks that collapsed into seconds until she could look out of the tiny window to see lights that went on forever.

And when she left the aircraft, mildly tiddly from the champagne she'd accepted during the flight, she had to follow other passengers for fear of getting lost in the immensity of the airport with its moving footpaths and innumerable signposts for the unwary, the innocent, the lost.

Then she emerged somehow into the public area of the airport and found Kurtis waiting, his sad eyes alight with pleasure, his smile welcoming, his hands outstretched for her own. And it was, as she had known it would be, just right.

'You might have told me you'd never flown before,' he said when they were driving away from the airport.

'And that I'd never been out of Tasmania in my life? Oh, you'd have loved that,' she replied, eyes drinking in his silhouette against the background of the city lights outside the car window.

'You'd have withdrawn your invitation quick-smart, I reckon. What would you want with a country girl in your life here?'

'Exactly what I've got,' he replied, turning his attention from the traffic long enough to scowl at her across the small interior of his Porsche.

Ruth found his face...different in the scatty light. Older, somehow, and yet younger too. Severe and yet, when the scowl transformed to a wondrously soft grin, so gentle it made her stomach flip, her very insides turn over.

Then the instant was over and he returned his attention to his driving until a red light gave him time to look at her once again. Which he did, a quirky grin playing round his mouth.

'I am extremely pleased, my lady witch, that you found it expedient to accept my humble invitation,' he said, then continued without giving Ruth any chance to reply, 'And while this humble chariot is, of course, a paltry vehicle compared to your incomparable broomstick, it is all I can offer for the moment.'

She laughed, accepting his overdone attempt to return their conversation to a lighter note.

''Twill suffice,' she replied then. 'Provided, of course, it allows you to pander to my tourist desires and point out all possible highlights *en route* to your castle.'

'Your wish, my lady witch, is my veritable command,' he replied with a grin, then returned his attention to the job of driving in traffic such as Ruth had never seen.

He drove her into a dream, the car's throaty exhaust sound punctuating visions Ruth had seen on television and in magazine advertisements, but never in their awesome reality. Sydney Harbour Bridge, smaller than she'd imagined but memorable for all of that. The opera house, also smaller, somehow, but so lovely in the night lights. The centre of the city, the canyons of streets between the cliffs of the tall, bright-lit buildings, the crowds, the traffic. Ruth felt truly the country bumpkin, oooing and aaahing, her eyes bright, her very being alive with the excitement——

Until, suddenly, she was plagued by yawns and her escort grinned his gentle grin and reached across to touch her wrist, his fingers like butterfly wings.

'I think 'tis time you called it a night, my lady witch. It would be nice if you had *some* strength left for the theatre tomorrow night.'

Ruth could only nod her acceptance; she could barely keep her eyes open, suddenly exhausted. By the time he parked the car she was sound asleep, her head on his shoulder, and she barely wakened sufficiently to be escorted into a waiting lift, then into a high-rise apartment that looked out over the night city as if from the height of an aeroplane.

'You sit here and I'll be back in a minute with your gear,' Kurtis said, smiling in the subdued light. He had to waken her again when he returned. 'You're fair whacked,' he whispered, lifting her into his arms and carrying her through to a large bedroom where a utilitarian daybed shared space with an army of computer gear that seemed to have spread like a gigantic mould. 'I just hope it's a quiet night,' he said, gently depositing Ruth on her feet. 'I daren't turn all this stuff off, so if you find yourself hearing all sorts of electronic grunts and groans just ignore them and go back to sleep.'

'I don't think *anything* could keep me awake,' she replied, already eyeing the bed with a sigh of welcome.

'Well, it might be noisier, but you're safer here than with me,' he grinned, and kissed her ever so gently before turning away to the door. 'Bathroom's first on the left and the kitchen's straight ahead. Sleep well, my lady witch, and I'll see you in the dawning.'

If he did, it could only have been a glimpse of a sleeping figure, because the next thing Ruth knew it was well past dawn and she was struggling up out of the deepest sleep she could remember in years. Throwing on her housecoat, she peered cautiously into the living-room to find her host sprawled in a balcony lounge chair with a newspaper on his knee and three others awaiting their turn.

'Afternoon,' he said with a grin that broadened at her half-shy nod. 'You'll want a shower and whatever, so why not get at it and I'll start breakfast?'

'I didn't mean to sleep so long,' Ruth replied, aware that she still wasn't quite awake. Was she really *here*? Really in Kurtis Goodwin's apartment ... in Sydney? It all seemed quite unreal and yet so ... comfortable.

'You must have needed it,' he replied, rising lithely to his feet. His hair was still damp, so he hadn't been up that long himself, she presumed. Just long enough to have showered and dressed in casual jeans and sweat-shirt and got his morning papers.

Comfortable, yet she shied like a nervous horse when he tilted her chin to touch her mouth with his lips, flinched at the closeness of him, the delicious taste of his mouth.

'I ... I'll have that shower, I think,' she stammered, turning quickly away, but not so quickly that she missed seeing the wry grin he tossed her.

'Coffee will be ready,' he laughed, turning towards the kitchen. And when she emerged ten minutes later, he had ready not only the coffee, but a huge bowl of fresh fruit, and he was busy stirring at something in a large mixing bowl.

'Pancakes or waffles, my lady?' he asked, eyes roving approval over her casual shorts and T-shirt, put on in deference to the unexpected warmth.

'For breakfast?'

'Of course. I realise you Australians eat them for dessert, which is a habit I find quite astonishing,' he replied. 'But I prefer them for breakfast, with heaps of butter and maple syrup and bacon, though I wouldn't dream of suggesting you have the bacon.'

'Just as well,' Ruth replied with a grimace. Then she remembered her manners. 'Waffles would be heavenly, but only after I've had two cups of coffee to prepare me.'

'As good as done.'

And it was. Delightfully so, and the more so since he proved to be a far superior cook to Ruth herself. Not, she admitted to him rather shamefully, that it would take much to accomplish that.

'Hardly surprising, considering you live on rabbit food,' he replied with a grin. 'Not real fair to expect gourmet cooking from a woman who won't eat the results. Or are you really that strict a vegetarian in the first place? It isn't something we've discussed, and it might be nice to know, in case I have to change our dinner reservation for tonight.'

'I'm not a fanatic about it,' Ruth said. 'I do eat fish and chicken occasionally; it's just red meat I'm not fond of, really.'

'That's all right, then,' he said. 'The place I've booked, we can do a bit of Jack Sprat manipulating and both end up well-satisfied.' He rose to pour them fresh coffee, then asked, 'But first—considering we have most of the day ahead of us—I suppose you'd like to play tourist?'

'Oh, yes, please. I want to see . . . well . . . everything.' And she knew he was seeing again the country bumpkin, but she didn't care, because the expression in his eyes was one of total approval, total acceptance.

And play tourist they did—with a vengeance! Kurtis had her out of the apartment almost before Ruth could think. The dishes could wait, he said. Everything could wait; his electronic office virtually ran itself and there was an answering machine—'three, actually'—to cover for him in his absence.

Hand in hand, they made the long, steep descent to the Mosman ferry terminal; hand in hand they rode the ferry into the city, Kurtis playing tour guide as they travelled; hand in hand they walked the inner-city streets, almost oblivious to the crowds, to almost everything except the city sights and each other.

Then they were on another ferry, this time to visit Taronga Park Zoo, then back to the city for a change of ferries and eventually back to where they'd started.

Ruth purely revelled in it all, taking in everything with a childlike wonder, a childlike delight. Kurtis, she thought, shed years in the single day. He laughed with her, at her, in spite of her. They laughed together.

And they returned to his flat, eventually, still alive with their adventure, closer than they'd ever been, somehow *together* in a fashion Ruth could never have imagined.

'And there's more to come,' he said as they paused over a quick coffee before changing for dinner and their theatre date. 'Not that I'm at all sure I can keep up, my lady witch. You set a fair pace for a geriatric to meet.'

'You're no more a geriatric than I am,' she replied, eyes shining, then twirled in a pirouette of sheer exuberance. 'The night is young...'

'And you're so beautiful.' He concluded the lines for her, hands moving to catch her, to stop her spinning, to draw her into his arms as if she belonged there. 'So very beautiful,' he sighed as his lips swept down to plunder her mouth with the same enthusiasm he'd exhibited throughout the day.

It was a kiss, yet more than a kiss, Ruth felt. It was a sort of celebration, a recognition of how wonderful their day together had been, still was, would be.

She melted into his embrace, her own pleasure merely heightened by his touch, by the taste of him, the touch of him. His fingers tumbled an erotic tune down her spine, met in the small of her back in that soft place where they could stroke slow, intimate fires that surged through her entire body.

Ruth found herself wondering at how superbly they fitted together, how he was exactly the right height to kiss her, exactly the right flavour for her, how her fingers so naturally reached the back of his neck, where the crispness of his hair felt just right.

His embrace tightened, flattening her breasts against the warmth of his chest, pulling her hips to him so that the evidence of his ardour was unmistakable, undeniable. His fingers were beneath her T-shirt now, his touch warm against her skin yet so light as to be almost ticklish.

Ruth could barely breathe, didn't care, didn't want to breathe. She wanted only for the kiss to go on forever, for his touch to go on forever. Her nipples had hardened against his chest, her entire body now replying to his caresses, her fingers tangled in his hair, holding his mouth as it claimed her own.

She could feel his fingers at her bra strap, sensed her body writhing to ease their task. And then—without warning—it was over; Kurtis had removed his fingers, eased the tightness of his embrace.

'Too soon, too late, too…something, my lady witch.' He shrugged, but his eyes glowed with a passion Ruth knew had matched her own, a need she had shared, had wanted to share.

Kurtis was stepping away from her now, though his hands had clasped her fingers to raise them to his lips and his eyes held her as firmly as a chain round her neck.

'I think it best you go and get changed now, lest we be late for dinner,' he said, his voice ragged with a passion she felt even through his light touch at her fingertips. 'There may be a time for this, *will* be a time, but it isn't now,' he added, and his voice revealed both regret and determination.

Ruth met his soft sad eyes, knowing that in doing so she could only reveal her willingness, her acceptance of his embraces, of his caress, his touch, his entire being. But if he sensed that, saw that, he revealed nothing; he merely smiled down into her eyes, then slowly released her fingers and waved her towards the hallway.

'First shower to you, my lady,' he whispered as she turned away, breathless with her own emotions and her confusion. 'I'll have mine while you get changed.'

Ruth, her thoughts as much a jumble as her emotions, plunged beneath the shower and stood, head bowed beneath the needles of water, unable to make any sense of it at all.

He wanted her; no argument there. And she, beyond any question, wanted him to want her, wanted him … it

was that simple. But something was holding him back;
something was interfering with his—their—situation.

Something as damned stupid as soaking her hair, she
realised with a start that turned to a chuckle and then
a heartfelt laugh. Going out in half an hour and here
she stood like a drowned rat; it would take all of that
to get her rowdy mane under sufficient control to look
anything like half decent.

She was still smiling at the idiocy of it all when she
passed him in the narrow passageway, her body wrapped
in one towel, her hair in another.

'I'm a fool,' she said with a shake of her head, 'but
it'll dry enough to tame before we get wherever we're
going. I hope.'

'There's one of those blow-dry things under the sink
in the vanity, if that's any help,' Kurtis replied with a
shake of his own head, the gesture revealing his
wonderment.

By the time she emerged from her room, wearing a
black evening skirt beneath a cream-coloured broderie
anglaise blouse, she had towelled her hair into the be-
ginnings of submission, and five minutes with the borrowed blow-drier completed the taming.

Kurtis, as she might have expected but for some reason
hadn't, was quite resplendent in evening wear, and his
expression at first sight of her, the warm glow that spread
from his eyes, forced a tiny lurch into her step. She
blamed it on the unaccustomed three-inch heel, but knew
better. She wanted to look good for him, wanted him to
feel comfortable with her appearance, to take pleasure
in it. She knew only too well that she lacked the money
or sophistication—or interest, to be honest—to meet
Sydney's dress standards, had never been sufficiently

interested in clothes to bother much about the latest styles and fashions.

Kurtis, of course, would have to. Power dressing, it was called, and she expected that in his line of work being properly turned out could be rather important. Or so she suspected; all she could think to say was, 'You look very nice.'

'As do you, my lady witch. Quite stunning, in fact,' he replied with a half-smile. 'Let us away and wow the peasants.'

Later, every second of that evening seemed to be burned into Ruth's consciousness, but while it was actually happening it seemed to flow in a river of sensation she never quite caught up with.

Their dinner was superb. Kurtis was obviously known at the restaurant he'd chosen, and everything about the dinner was splendid beyond expectation.

The theatre was pure delight, the performance far exceeding anything described in the review he'd thoughtfully kept for her from the newspaper critique. Ruth was so enthralled she hardly spoke, even during the interval; her mind just kept replaying the scenes over and over and over.

And when it was over she could only smile up at Kurtis as they left the theatre, her eyes smiling, her entire person at that perfect pitch of excitement.

'Shall we go on somewhere for a drink, supper?'

'No, thank you. Anything more would be...too much, if you know what I mean,' she replied. 'Let's just go...'

'Home? You need only ask and it shall be done,' he replied. And so they did, to arrive in the midst of what Ruth could only think of as utter chaos.

They entered the apartment to a cacophony of ringing bells and clattering electronic equipment and flashing lights that brought Ruth to an immediate and confused halt in the doorway, her first thought that what she was hearing was some sort of burglar alarm.

Kurtis was more astute. 'There goes the rest of our evening, I suspect,' he muttered, easing her through into the apartment so that he could slide past her and make his way to *her* room, from whence the bulk of the excitement seemed to originate.

Ruth could only follow, then stand, stalled, in the doorway. The room was an electronic nightmare, technology gone mad! Everywhere she looked, it seemed, machines were humming or clattering or hissing, with paper slithering into one machine, out of another, one telephone beeping, another ringing, a third silently flashing an imperative light.

Kurtis seemed unimpressed. 'You'll be sleeping in my bed tonight,' he muttered, turning to look down at Ruth's confusion. 'But you'll be there alone, from the look of this. Which is probably just as well. Come and we'll get that sorted out before I throw myself into working gear and get stuck into this.'

Ruth followed as he hefted her luggage and strode down the hall to deposit it in what was obviously the master bedroom of the apartment. Without speaking, he stripped off his dinner-jacket and began undoing his shirt, only to turn suddenly and look at Ruth as if surprised to see her there.

'Any chance you could put on some coffee while I change?' he asked, obviously distracted, his attention divided between Ruth and the chaos in the other bedroom. 'Then I'll be out of here and you can change, too, if you like.'

He emerged wearing faded jeans and a sweatshirt just as the electric jug boiled, and his smile, although sincere enough, was again touched by the distractions in his mind.

'You're a darling,' he said, reaching out to take the coffee-cup she offered. 'And I should be shot for not realising this would happen now, just when I've got you where I want you.'

He put the cup down, then reached out to take her hands and draw her nearer.

'I'm sorry, Ruth the witch, sorrier than you can imagine. But as of now you're on your own, I'm afraid, because the rest of our night together is going to be spent apart. There are some tricky little goings-ons in Eastern Canada that must, unfortunately, take priority even over romance.'

'Can I help?' she asked, knowing even as she spoke that it was probably a stupid question, so she was relieved by his grinning reply.

'Only by keeping quiet and out of the way for as long as it takes to sort out. I'm afraid this business is beyond even your powers, my lady witch. Although it would be appreciated if you feel like making some proper coffee. We're going to need it, I suspect.'

'Of course.' But he wasn't listening, had turned away to pluck up the kitchen telephone, the only one in the place not somehow connected to some sort of gadgetry.

'Ro? Trouble in French Canada, I'm sorry to say. Right, quick as you can; that's a good girl,' he said when the phone was answered, apparently on the first ring. He finished speaking, hung up, and turned back to lift

Ruth's chin so that he could drop a gentle, almost-but-not-quite impersonal kiss on her astonished lips.

'You're a good girl too,' he said with a grin—and was gone, striding into the office-bedroom with the air of a man going into battle.

Ruth stood for a moment, silent, astonished at the pace and speed of whatever was going on. Then she swiftly took herself off to his bedroom and got herself changed into clothing more suitable for whatever role she'd be involved in.

She came back within minutes in her own casual clothes, stifling a yawn as she peeped into the office-bedroom to see Kurtis striding from one fax machine to another, obviously deep in concentration, obviously not wanting to be disturbed. Ruth withdrew, returned to the kitchen and began scrounging through cupboards to find his percolator and the right sort of coffee to go with it.

She was on her hands and knees, prowling through a lower cupboard, when a husky, unfamiliar voice—a woman's voice—startled her beyond reason by saying, 'Try the freezer; that's where the coffee'll be.'

Ruth spun round on her knees to find herself staring up at one of the most beautiful women she had ever seen, an utter vision of sophisticated city elegance from nut-brown hair to the heels of shoes that must have cost a month's wages—for Ruth.

Elegant. There was no other word to describe the woman. Except perhaps exquisite. All the other trite little words like classically beautiful, lovely, striking, stylish—they all seemed just inadequate. Actually the face wasn't quite classically beautiful, but it certainly was elegant. The figure was near perfection, indeed perfect for the designer jersey dress that clung just right in all the right places. The bright green eyes that looked down at Ruth were calm, assured, seemed to hold just a touch of... amusement? Whatever, it was sufficient to make Ruth want to crawl into the open cupboard and hide.

A perfectly manicured hand reached down to grip hers, to lift her upwards in a helpful gesture that was somehow more commanding than helpful. Ruth still had to look up; the woman was easily three inches taller.

'I'm Rosemary Shimmin,' the terribly cultured voice said, every syllable suggesting it was a name Ruth should somehow know, would certainly never forget. 'And you, I presume,' said the woman in tones that combined condescension and patronising in a skilful blend, 'will be the witch person Kurtis has been raving about.'

CHAPTER THREE

ONLY when Ruth was on her feet did the woman put the keys in her other hand away in her expensive handbag, and something about the gesture made it more of a message than it needed to be.

These are *my* keys to *his* apartment, Rosemary Shimmin might as well have shouted. And I don't just have them for business, either, phoney witch. I've got them, I had them before you and I'll have them after you and don't you forget it.

Except that it was nowhere as blatant as that. Indeed, the message was subtle, very subtle. Exquisitely, elegantly subtle. But very, very clear for all of that.

Rosemary then spent a moment to brief Ruth on the kitchen, once again illustrating the boundaries of her prior claim, before stalking on splendid legs to join Kurtis in the office.

The night stretched—uncomfortably for Ruth—from that moment. She kept the coffee going, found ingredients to make toast, small nibbles of the type found at cocktail parties, huge sandwiches. The talk from the office-bedroom meant nothing to her; the intimacy so obvious between her host and Rosemary Shimmin at first bothered her, then became a matter of indifference. Rosemary's delicate sniping, which Kurtis was surely oblivious to in his concentration on the work at hand, was less easy to keep at arm's length, at times almost

56

impossible to ignore. But it was equally impossible to counter.

Clearly the two had a business relationship; it would have been impossible, Ruth knew, for it to be a platonic one. There were too many signs of that other sort of intimacy, too many small touchings, too many personal comments too intimate to mean anything but what they did mean. This woman had been involved with Kurtis, most likely still was involved, and definitely meant to continue that involvement.

Kurtis himself seemed unaware of the friction between the two women. He was so deeply involved in whatever business was afoot that he barely recognised Ruth except as a presence in the kitchen, and Rosemary appeared little more than another piece of office equipment in the circumstances.

Ruth, with some experience as an operating theatre nurse behind her, recognised that element of the situation with no trouble. She could see that Rosemary, despite her elegance, despite her stunning beauty, was really doing little more than supplying Kurtis with the office equivalent of forceps, clamps, scissors, sutures.

And, she quickly realised, the older woman *knew* Ruth could see that—and didn't much like it. The enormous, improbably green eyes gradually began to take on an expression that couldn't entirely be blamed on the lateness of the hour.

As the tension grew, Ruth thought seriously of simply packing up and getting out. She could take a cab, find a relatively inexpensive hotel somewhere, simply take herself out of the apartment, away from the aura of hostility Kurtis didn't seem to notice but which was increasing, becoming almost unbearable.

The moment came, but she missed it, was just too tired herself to seize the instant when an idle comment from Rosemary might have given her the chance. Ruth was fading fast and knew it, could hardly imagine how Kurtis seemed to grow visibly fresher as the night progressed with its interminable flurry of fax machines and photocopiers and strident telephones. But he did, and to her great surprise he managed to be aware of her own exhaustion as well.

'You want to be in bed, my lady witch,' he murmured as he sipped his umpteenth cup of strong coffee with one ear cocked towards the activity in the office behind him. 'I'm really sorry about this,' he added quietly. 'It wasn't part of the plan, I can assure you, but it also isn't anything I can ignore, either. You've been a wondrous help, more than you might realise, but that, too, wasn't part of the bargain. Why don't you wander off to bed? We've got quite a day tomorrow—today—before your plane goes, and if I get just a touch lucky I might get this all sorted out in time to play tourist again.'

'If you get at all lucky, you'll be spending the day in bed, asleep,' Ruth replied. 'Both of us will, I expect.'

Which provoked a wry grin. 'Together would be asking just a bit too much, I suppose,' he said, and chuckled at whatever look the comment must have put in her eyes. 'Fear not, my lady witch,' he said then. 'Timing, for any warlock, is almost everything—even for us apprentice-grade types. You'll be safe enough, I warrant, even if you should wake at dawn's early light to find me snuggled up beside you.'

'Safer than you, sir warlock,' Ruth finally managed to reply, her head fuzzy, her eyes slumping in tiredness. 'There are spells to cover such situations, and I'm so tired now I might make a mistake and use one a bit more long-lasting than would suit your future.'

His reply was a quick, light kiss on the forehead with an embrace that was so fleeting as to be non-existent, except that it somehow got her turned round and headed down the hall to his bedroom. As she went, she thought for an instant that she heard him mutter, 'You may already have,' but it was so indistinct that she entered the bedroom unsure if she'd really heard it or not, and less sure what it might have meant if she had.

'I'll just grab a quick catnap,' she said to herself as she sprawled on the king-sized bed, flipping a corner of the eiderdown coverlet over her legs as she did so. It must have been a sun-loving cat, because when she woke it was to find the late morning sun pouring through the window and Kurtis Goodwin—as promised—snuggled up beside her.

Ruth found herself tensing with an instinctive yet somehow quite illogical alarm, then as quickly relaxed and raised herself on one elbow so that she could look down and watch the sleeping man beside her.

In slumber, he looked younger, somehow. The closed eyes revealed nothing of their world-weariness, the strong lines that normally bracketed his mobile mouth were softened, the tousled hair could have been any age, but for the shadings of grey.

Easing herself from the bed gingerly, so as not to disturb him, Ruth tiptoed over and quietly closed the heavy curtains, then returned to stand beside the bed, once again looking at Kurtis.

Handsome indeed, she decided, although certainly not in any conventional way. She was turning away, her mind already ahead of her in the kitchen, with the need for coffee, when she was caught by the wrist and dragged back to land upon the bed with a small shriek of surprise.

The shriek faded out as she found herself somehow lying within the cradle of Kurtis's arms, almost nose to nose with the man she'd been so sure was asleep.

'Caught, my lady witch?'

His eyes laughed at her; his mouth was twisted in a merry grin even as his fingers trailed a melody along her spine.

Ruth could only stare. Words leapt to her lips only to die in the dryness there, a dryness she knew wouldn't last much longer, would be moistened by his kiss. Must be!

'If you're always this frisky in the morning, it's back to the old cauldron for another stir,' she eventually managed to reply. 'This is no time for such antics, warlock or not.'

'Antics?' One eyebrow raised in a quizzical, mocking gesture. 'Here I've been trying to get you into my bed for weeks and when you get here you think it's *antics*?'

'What else? After the night you've put in, I can't imagine you being serious,' Ruth replied, lying through her teeth. He was serious enough and she knew it, actually hoped for it. Except that she was afraid of it, too.

'It was a good night. Got heaps done, solved problems, and now we have the day—or what's left of it—to enjoy ourselves,' he replied with a hungry-eyed grin. 'And what better place to start than here?' His hands never stopped stroking the small of her back, and as he spoke his eyes caressed her face, touched her eyes, her nose, slid down the curve of her cheek, rested briefly on her mouth to ready it for his kiss.

Ruth was torn between wanting to lean into his kiss and wanting—needing—to put some distance between them. Now. Now, before it was too late forever.

And then, as if from some magic mirror, the image of Rosemary Shimmin floated up between them, green eyes laughing at Ruth, perfectly painted lips curled in a sneer of derision.

It was enough! Ruth rolled herself out of his arms, her feet thudding into the bedroom carpet as she almost broke into a run. This was no place for her, and, although her heart cried out in despair at the leaving, her common sense cheered her on.

'I need coffee,' she cried over her shoulder, 'and...and the loo.'

And you, she thought as she made it to the doorway and turned to see Kurtis lying back on one elbow, his eyes following her with a vaguely bemused expression. And you, but not like this, not now, not here. And she shut the door firmly behind her before she could change her mind.

It was no comfort at all to find the kitchen spotless, all the dishes and glasses washed and put away, all traces of the long night's foraging removed. Score one more for the elegant Rosemary, Ruth thought, and started to mess it up all over again.

Not a sign of the woman remained in the apartment, and yet, somehow, her presence was all-pervasive. Ruth fancied she could still smell Rosemary's perfume, could almost still hear her voice.

Kurtis didn't appear by the time the coffee was perked, the toast made. Ruth debated, then slunk down the corridor and peeped in to see him sprawled across his bed, obviously asleep despite his earlier, momentary friskiness.

Ruth drank her coffee and ate the toast, but her mind was on neither activity. She felt...somehow cheated. Not by his working through the night; she was adult enough to accept that such was a logical part of his working structure. And not, really, by the presence of the elegant woman who was so obviously a part of his work—and his life.

'And you lie, especially to yourself,' she muttered aloud, knowing it was true, knowing she *did* resent Rosemary's involvement, did resent the woman's presence in *her* weekend. But then Ruth grinned, had to grin, remembering that everything about Rosemary had screamed out that *she* resented Ruth just as much.

'I suppose I ought to be flattered,' Ruth chuckled to herself. And wondered why she wasn't. Just as she wondered, hours later, why she'd allowed Kurtis to sleep right through until it was time to take her to the airport.

'I feel abominably guilty about this,' he said grumpily as they drove to the airport. 'After all, my lady witch, my entire warlock's reputation has come adrift. I'd be lucky to maintain even my apprentice grading after this fiasco.'

'You did what you promised,' Ruth replied calmly, almost too cool, she thought. 'You provided bed and board and dinner and the theatre, exactly to plan.'

'There was more to the plan than that, and well you know it,' he replied. 'I never even got to recite "The Highwayman" to you, and I was quite looking forward to that. Ah, well...perhaps next time.'

But it wasn't until her boarding call that he turned her into his arms to declare, rather than ask, 'There will be a next time, Ruth the witch. And it will be soon, I promise you.'

'I'd like that,' Ruth replied, truthfully enough. 'And thank you very much for *this* time. I really enjoyed it.' Which was stretching the truth just a little bit, but after all, she thought, wasn't that a witch's privilege?

During the flight home, she found herself wishing that somehow she could really be a witch, could really cast spells. Because then, just maybe, she could find a spell to rid her mind of Rosemary's taunting eyes and haughty, sniping comments.

Kurtis, apparently, had never doubted. She was still very much a witch to him, if his next letter was anything to go by. It arrived less than a week later, thanking her for blessing his castle with her presence and apologising for the various inconveniences caused by his business dealings. All very flowery, very tongue-in-cheek, but all the more delightful for it. No mention, of course, of Rosemary, not that Ruth would have expected any.

He would be coming to Hobart, he said, within the week. Which would give her time to finish whatever ghastly brew she might be stewing, polish her gap teeth and please, please, please to do something about that hair.

He might, the gods and Telecom permit it, even go so far as to telephone her beforehand, he suggested, humbly begging her pardon for not doing so already.

And on the Thursday night he did phone, from some place Ruth had never heard of in a far-flung corner of western Queensland. She had a second letter by then, just as flowery as the first and even more astonishing in that, like the first, it had no return address, but somehow assumed she had replied to the first letter, and proceeded to answer her never-written reply.

And such a reply it must have been! Her new-found warlock—with the greatest of humility, of course—professed to have been thoroughly smitten by it, and went on from there. Combined with the first letter, it was sufficient to have her quite thoroughly confused when his voice rasped over the telephone, 'Art well, my lady witch?'

'Well enough to be satisfied with my hair the way it is,' she replied, grasping at the first thing which came to mind, then wishing she hadn't, because the sniping comment brought with it an involuntary vision of Rosemary's shimmering, ever-so-neat cap of nut-brown hair. 'What are you trying to do anyway, convert me to a mere human?'

'I? With my puny and minuscule apprentice powers? Oh, you wrong me, my lady. I did but *suggest*.'

'You're lucky I don't turn you into a...a...' His laughter made it impossible to continue.

'Can you wait until tomorrow night?'

'If I must. Where are you this time, or shouldn't I ask?'

'Melbourne. Can you make us a dinner booking somewhere posh for about ten? Leave it flexible, in case the airlines don't recognise your powers and I'm a bit late.'

'All right,' she said, not at all sure that it really was. 'But perhaps you could be a bit more specific about what you consider "posh".'

'Somewhere that will feed you your rabbit food and still be fancy enough to demand that you wear legs,' he replied. 'If possible, somewhere we can dance, my lady witch, for I've an almost indecent desire to take you in my arms and whirl us both to the stars.'

'I don't dance.' An impulsive admission, but one best made now, she decided.

'Don't, won't or can't?' he asked. 'I wouldn't have thought there was much you couldn't do, somehow.'

'I never learned and I've got horrible co-ordination,' Ruth replied, then hurried on, trying to both change the subject and ask before she forgot, 'Do you want me to pick you up at the airport?'

'Waiting at airports is among the most fruitless occupations in the world,' he said. 'Wait for me at home, where you can curl up with a good book or do something useful.'

'I quite like airports,' she replied. Her first lie, and quickly regretted, but only because she suddenly realised how eager it must make her sound. What would he think—that she was so impatient for his company she couldn't wait? 'I . . . I enjoy the opportunity for people-watching,' she hurriedly added.

'Then pander to your enjoyment by all means,' he replied with a laugh. 'I'll be there about nine, flying Ansett. You're sure you don't mind?'

'I wouldn't have offered if I did,' Ruth replied. 'But I do wonder if you want to be raging about at that late an hour when you've been travelling so much.'

'I've told you before,' he growled, 'I'm not a geriatric. But I am open to reasonable offers. What do you suggest—tea and biccies beside a bubbling cauldron? Followed by . . . ?'

And his voice was so, so suggestive that Ruth found herself unable to reply until after a noticeable and revealing pause.

'Too fast? Ah, well, it's one of my failings, dear lady witch. One of many, indeed. I shall probably settle down as I get older. See you at the airport.'

And he was gone, abruptly as usual but somehow without seeming discourteous in the process. Ruth found herself holding a silent telephone and staring off into space.

She arrived at the airport the next evening with a sudden, terrifying thought that she might not recognise him, and had to shake herself at the sheer idiocy of the idea. It seemed quite strange, however, to be waiting in the arrivals lounge all dressed up for an evening out.

But it was worth it to see the light in his eyes as he stalked into the lounge and swept his gaze over her before setting down his luggage and bowing over her hand.

'My lady witch,' he murmured formally. But his eyes said volumes and his touch even more. It was as if they'd never been apart; he took her hand and the thrill of it shot through her body like a lightning bolt.

Kurtis looked both exhausted and elated, as if he'd been running on his nerves for far, far too long. But Ruth said nothing, certain he would ignore her concerns. Or, worse, misinterpret them.

He left her in the Sheraton's Atrium bar while he went to shower and change, returning with damp hair and a fresh shave.

'Right! Now I'm ready for anything...or almost anything,' he said. 'Shall we away, my lady?'

Ruth learned that evening that she *could* dance, and more important that her feeling of contentment in Kurtis's company hadn't been just an illusion. Throughout the evening she found herself more and more drawn to him, more and more comfortable with him, more and more delighted with his zany sense of humour, his sardonic wit. Even his intensity seemed muted in the magic of the night—until the witching hour struck, and with it Ruth's punishment for her temerity at calling herself a witch.

'Will you have a waterfall for me tomorrow?' he asked out of a long silence in which she had been floating in his arms and dreaming...of waterfalls.

'I...you've got a nerve calling *me*, a witch,' she said with a start. 'Sometimes I think you read my mind.'

'I can but try,' he grinned, easing the distance between them so that he could meet her eyes. 'But actually it's your body I read; a very expressive body it is, too. But you haven't answered my question.'

'I could...find one, I suppose,' she finally said, finding it difficult to speak, even to think, under the mesmerising intensity of his gaze.

'I don't suppose there's one relatively handy that you haven't already seen yourself,' he said. 'It would be nice for both of us to see something new.'

'I'll sleep on it,' she promised.

'Hardly fair,' was the smiling, teasing response. 'I sleep and dream of you, and you dream of waterfalls. How am I going to get you to the altar with that attitude?'

'Witches don't marry; you should know that,' she replied lightly, hoping he hadn't felt the curious little lurch in her heart just at having him *jest* about marriage. Too soon, too soon. 'Besides,' she heard herself adding, 'the way you live you don't have time to be married.'

It was supposed to be a light-hearted remark; Kurtis's response was anything but.

'Well, it certainly wouldn't be anything like conventional marriages I've seen. I can tell you that from past experience,' he said. 'Also, from past experience, I'd about decided to finish my life without trying marriage again. It must be the spell you've cast on me, Ruth, because I've been thinking more than seriously about it just lately.'

'Well, you shouldn't be,' she replied staunchly. 'An apprentice-grade warlock has no business with such thoughts. Think of your career, of how many centuries of study and toil lie ahead.'

Kurtis was silent; he swirled her back into his arms and spent the next several minutes blending her with the music, his fingers at her back guiding her in the dance and making love to her at the same time. Ruth could only flow with his movements, her mind drunk with his touch, intoxicated by the smoothness of his movements, the way his body seemed to merge into her own as the music carried them.

Shortly afterwards, they left, and after Kurtis had handed her into the car and slid himself into the passenger seat he reached out to take her hand, drawing her round to face him.

'Take me home with you, Ruth,' he said. 'I want to see where you live, how you live. My only mental pictures of you are beside refrigerators and waterfalls, and I need more to sustain me in my wanderings.'

'I...' she began, then halted, could only stare at him, her body singing to his touch but her mind screaming untold dangers.

'Surely you can't fear a mere apprentice-grade warlock,' he whispered, his fingers sliding up her wrist to touch like velvet in the crook of her elbow. His eyes seemed to glow in the half-light, reaching out to touch at her throat, at her lips, pleading and demanding as one.

'Coffee,' she whispered in reply, half of her hating even that much surrender. 'I'll give you coffee, but you can't...stay.'

'Oh, my lady witch. Nothing could be further from my mind,' he denied, sliding into his warlock role but never removing the brand of his eyes and his touch. 'Even had I the temerity to suggest such a thing, would a humble warlock dare risk being turned to a...?'

'A cane toad,' she muttered, finally summoning the strength to turn from him and start the car. 'And don't you forget it!'

'Upon my honour,' he swore. And stuck to it. They drove to her flat, which was duly admired, she made coffee and they drank it in an atmosphere so thick with sexual tension, Ruth could hardly breathe. His every move, his every gesture, his every look was a declaration of intent. He didn't have to say he wanted her body; she knew it, almost welcomed it. Did welcome it, but feared it more, and he seemed to know that, seemed almost to delight in making his declaration both a statement of safety and a promise for later.

'It isn't the time, Ruth. Yet. But the time will come, and when it does...' he said, then he had her call him a taxi and returned to his hotel. Her only danger was the lingering after-effects of a goodnight kiss that promised heaven and hell and everything between.

He returned promptly at eight in a hire car and they had breakfast *en route* to National Park, where they visited the ever-popular Russell Falls, then moved on towards Maydena and the walk up to the base of Marriotts

Falls, which was equally spectacular in its own way, buried as it was in a dense rainforest gully.

Ruth had chosen to wear shorts and an oversized T-shirt, with no need for a bra because of the warmth of the day, and once again was only too aware of Kurtis's eyes as she walked ahead of him through the tall ferns and taller trees. Only now it was a pleasing sensation, and she made no move to stilt her long, free stride, only took pleasure in his obvious admiration. It was...just good.

And at the end of their journey—this one only an hour's return walk—was the most idyllic setting.

Water streamed down enormous black rock cliffs, spreading in a million tiny rivulets as it did so, then landing in a small pond formed by boulders from when part of the cliff had fallen away in the distant past. Ruth had her boots off in an instant; she just *had* to wade in the pool, *had* to experience the spray of the water as it tumbled down the glistening faces of the rock.

So entranced was she by the setting that she didn't even notice Kurtis taking pictures—hadn't noticed him with a camera, for that matter—until she turned back to grin at him with her eyes shining and her hands out-stretched in a gesture of wonder at the beauty of the place.

Then, apprehensive of having her photo taken, she lost the spontaneity of the moment, and he responded by putting the small camera back in his pocket.

'Are you going to be my lady witch, or perhaps my lady of the waterfalls?' he asked her when she returned, almost shyly now, to join him where he sat on a huge boulder.

'Oh, definitely your witch,' she replied. 'Although I do like waterfalls. But only a witch can cast spells.'

'Don't you believe it. If it comes out, I'll have a picture that proves waterfalls can put spells upon witches...just you wait and see.'

'Nobody's ever taken a decent picture of me in my entire life,' she said, thinking as she did so that it wasn't only waterfalls that could cast spells on her. Kurtis was doing a fair job of it all by himself.

'Ah, but maybe nobody's ever seen you the way I do,' he said. And his eyes fairly glowed as they toured her face, her body. 'In this picture, you'll emerge as a water-witch, captured by the camera at worship. It will be beautiful, you'll see.'

Which perhaps she would, but just at that moment her mind was captured more by the way he looked at her, the way he seemed to see through her defences, to see the way she was feeling. He stripped her with his eyes, but it was a slow, sensuous, delicate process that seemed, if anything, too slow, too tantalising.

As was his kiss, when he lifted her from the pool with her clothes and hair and skin all a-glisten with tiny drop-lets of spray. His lips touched her mouth, then traversed her face, mopping up the droplets, it seemed, one by one.

Beneath the T-shirt her breasts thrust against him, teased firm by the enchantment of the waterfall and the sudden warmth of his body after the coolness of the spray. As his lips returned to her mouth, his kiss deep-ening, he moved his fingers into her dampened, rowdy hair, pulling her against him as he drank from her mouth, as their bodies merged in this primeval glade with a sudden, primitive passion.

'Witch or water-witch; it's all the same,' he gasped some centuries later, lifting his head from where his lips had sipped her breasts to throbbing, lifting one hand from where it had been lazily tracing patterns of ecstasy along the lengths of her bare thighs as she lay across his lap where he sprawled atop a gigantic boulder.

Ruth's mind at that moment had been barely able to comprehend his words; it had merged with her body in a foaming waterfall of unheralded delight and wonder at his kisses, his touch...

She squirmed in her chair, lulled by memory and the fire's warmth into forgetting that she didn't *want* memories like that, didn't *want* anything of Kurtis, didn't want him, couldn't handle him, couldn't stop loving him... and hating him.

The knock at her door had to be repeated before she heard and comprehended it, so lost was she in her head. Ruth leapt to her feet, threw a fearful glance at the witch in the mirror as she swept past, and flung open the door to recoil just as precipitately, eyes widened with shock, her body poised for flight but with nowhere to go.

Kurtis met her startled eyes, standing comfortably, one dark eyebrow raised as his searching eyes roamed over her, taking in her dishevelled hair, her wide, staring eyes, the housecoat that gaped to reveal more breast than it concealed.

'Afraid, my lady witch?' he asked in that ever-familiar gravelly voice. 'Surely not, and for what possible reason? I've only come to talk to you, or have you been reading things into my letters again that were never existent?'

Then his hand was on her elbow, and she was being turned through the doorway, led into the hallway of her own home like a stranger. Ruth heard the door snick behind them, but her attention was focused entirely on the man whose touch burned at her arm like a torch. As they passed the hall mirror she caught a fleeting glimpse of herself, wild-eyed, wild-haired, truly witch-like, and of Kurtis, urbane, sophisticated, totally self-contained as always.

She yanked her arm free as they reached the doorway to the living-room, flinging herself ahead of him and standing—harridan-like and not caring a whit—to defy him, to deny him entry if she could; knowing she couldn't.

'I haven't read anything into your letter!' she cried. 'I haven't even *read* your letter. And I don't want to, either. I was going to just burn it; I almost did.'

He merely shrugged, shaking his head in a gesture that conveyed sadness rather than anger.

'Well, how about you point me at the kitchen and I'll make us some coffee while you *do* read the damned thing?' he finally asked.

Anything! she thought. Anything but having to stand there with Kurtis looking at her from those sad, knowing eyes, looking into her, through her.

She pointed mutely towards the kitchen and spun away from him, scurrying to her chair and hustling to close up her robe securely before she curled up with her legs tucked beneath her.

Read the letter! Damn the letter . . . and then Kurtis Goodwin for writing it, for sending it, for . . . everything, she thought. And she picked up the single sheet of paper.

'Dear my lady witch . . .' The words swam before her eyes, and she reached absently for her glasses, the ones he always said gave her the look of a myopic owl.

The time has come to stop running, Ruth. If you want to be free, I'll let you go, but unless you're ready to face up to what's going wrong between us you never will be free—you'll just be running.

I can't let you do that. I love you too much, difficult though it may be for you to believe...

Ruth spun her head round to glare at him as Kurtis silently placed a cup of coffee beside her.

'You can't stop me. You can't and you know it,' she hissed. 'There is nothing you can do to stop me. Nothing!'

'Just finish the letter,' Kurtis replied wearily, taking his own coffee and going to sit across the room on the shabby sofa.

Ruth followed him with her eyes, willing him to sit as far from her as possible, willing him *not* to look at her, not watch her as she returned to the letter.

We have to talk about this—not in fancy, flowery words like I've always used to write to you, but in real words to deal with a real problem.

I will be there Friday, by which time you should have this letter. And if I'm allowed any choice in the matter, we *will* talk about this, talk it until we can't talk any more, if necessary.

For your own sake if not mine—ours—please talk to me, Ruth. Please just give us one last try at actually communicating like adults.

'There's nothing to talk about!' Ruth fairly spat that remark at him, unnerved by the simplicity of the letter, by how much it said, and yet how little. But mostly by his stark declaration of love. 'And I'm not running, either,' she insisted, forcing herself to meet his raised eyebrow, the downturned quirk of his lips that silently shouted back her lie.

'You ran,' he said, 'like a rabbit. And, with hindsight, I'm not sure I blame you, either.'

'You know where you can put your hindsight,' she snapped angrily. 'Sideways!'

Again that raised eyebrow, along with a slight shake of his head that implied amused tolerance. It served only to make Ruth even wilder.

'You shouldn't be here,' she shouted. 'I didn't ask you to come; I didn't want you to come. I didn't...'

'You ran like a rabbit,' he repeated. 'Which is what I think surprised me more than anything about all this. You're not a quitter, Ruth. You've never been a quitter. But you ran and from the sound of you you're still running and I just...don't...know...why.'

Because of you, she wanted to shout. Because you took me into your life like some stray waif and you gave me everything and you said you loved me but all the time you were laughing at me.

But she didn't say it. Didn't say anything, because he was *looking* at her like that, with that curious glimmer in his eyes that had always had the ability to melt her insides, to make her shimmer like summer lightning. In the earliest days of their wildfire relationship, she'd been able to survive the days without him just on the strength of that look.

Unbidden, her mind slid back to her earlier reverie and the slow, leisurely drive back from Marriotts Falls. The entire return journey had been an exploration, a teasing, tantalising foretaste of what both must have known was to come.

Ruth had driven—carefully, almost sedately, trying to enjoy the touch of his fingers on her thigh without giving in to the fierce desire she had had to stop the car and fling herself into his arms. Just occasionally, she would risk a sideways glance, always to find those amazing eyes drinking her in, his gaze as focused as his touch.

His fingers had never stopped in their endless wanderings, sometimes lingering on her knee, sometimes on the soft inner skin of her thigh, from where warm rays had shot to the centre of her being.

'You *must* stop that,' she had protested once. 'You'll have us in the ditch.'

'I can't,' he had whispered. 'And I won't. You just pay attention to your driving, my lady witch, and ignore it.'

Ignore it? As easy ignore the lowering sun from which they fled. As easy ignore life itself. With all possible attention focused on her driving, she was still, Ruth had thought, a certifiable menace on the road.

And when they had reached her flat, he had somehow managed to maintain that marvellous, astonishing tension of promise. He had insisted she must have coffee, and made her some; he had insisted she must rest her eyes, only to whisper seductively in her ear as she obeyed.

When he had finally guided her to the bedroom, it was as if she floated inches above the floor. When he had carefully stripped away her T-shirt, eased away the rest of her clothing, his lips had followed his busy fingers, laying a path of kisses down her entire body.

There was never a question, now. This was the time, and it was the right time. It had seemed hours, days, while he kissed her, stroked her, tasted her, before he allowed their bodies to merge and begin the build-up to the whirlwind. No shyness had hampered their love-making, no sense of worry or guilt. Ruth had sent her fingers on explorations of their own, allowed herself—gifted herself—with just the sense of adventure and wonder he had created in her.

He had taken her to the heights of release, held her there for an infinity, then plunged with her in a dizzying tumble through ecstasy. And moments later, resting on one elbow but still without leaving her, he had done it again—simply with that *look* and the gentlest touch of his fingers beneath her ear. Only the beginning...

And now he was doing it again! Ruth shook her head as if to destroy the look with pure energy, as if she could thwart its effects by blurring her own vision.

'Stop that! Stop it,' she cried, lurching from her chair and fleeing to stand staring out of the kitchen window, seeking refuge in the grey skies and rain, refuge from memory, from pain.

'Only if you stop running,' he said. 'But no, not even then. I love you, Ruth; I have from the very beginning and I can't stop now.'

'Love!' She spat the word at him, turning wide-eyed to glare across to where he sat, patient as always, watching. 'You don't know the meaning of the word. It's all just a game to you, a cruel, evil *game*! Your letters, your phone calls, everything. Just a game!'

That got to him. She took some small delight in the wave of shock that flowed across his features. Saw him surge to his feet, anger a ripple that surged through his clenched jaw muscles.

'My letters, Ruth, may have been fanciful and they may have been verbose and they may even have been—

heaven help me—too damned prone to hiding my feelings in pretty words. But they were never a game. Never.'

And now he was stalking towards her, crossing the room like some great jungle cat. Ruth scurried in retreat, moving in counterpoint to maintain furniture between them. But when he reached the window where she'd been staring out, he halted, and himself looked out to the rain.

Ruth found herself back beside her chair, her knees so weak she could barely stand. She sank into it with a sigh of relief, only to recoil as he moved to loom beside her.

'Your coffee's cold; I'll make some more,' he said quietly, and had picked up the cup and gone before she could even decide if she wanted more. Swivelling in the chair, she watched him moving deftly through her kitchen, his every movement so economic and self-contained, and so familiar.

He brought the coffee, returned to his former seat. Then sat, cloaked in silence and staring into the fresh coffee he'd brought for himself. When he finally did look at her, that look was gone from his eyes; they seemed merely sad, almost empty.

'You used to like my letters,' he said in a voice that was whisper-soft, yet seemed to leap across the room at her.

Like them? She had literally *lived* for those letters, both during their all-too-brief courtship and beyond, beyond into the strange new world of marriage with a man who was seldom home, who spent his time in the whirlybird world of corporate high finance, coming home only to recharge his batteries with long walks and lovemaking.

'Dear my lady witch...' The words lay like a brand in her vision as Ruth picked up his letter again, reading the words as if for the first time. She read it, reread it.

'Are you trying to say I'm not an adult?' she demanded, her voice hoarse with aggression, fuelled by an anger she had to keep stoking from deep inside her. Had to... lest she lose all, everything now.

'I said we have to try and communicate like adults,' he replied. Calm... too calm.

'It's the same thing,' she insisted. 'It implies...'

'It implies nothing,' he snapped. 'It says what it says. But for God's sake, Ruth, look at us. We're sniping at each other here like children in the playground.'

'*My* playground,' she retorted. 'And one, I remind you, to which you were *not* invited.'

Eyes like stone returned her stare. Then he shrugged, shook his head wearily.

'How about you go put on some clothes, Ruth?' he asked quietly. 'We'll go somewhere and eat—I'm starved if you aren't—and maybe in neutral surroundings we can start making some sense.'

'I'm not hungry.' A child's sulky response; she knew it and instantly regretted it.

'You can't keep putting this off forever,' Kurtis said, voice bland but his eyes now touching her in tangible caresses at her lips, her throat, the deep opening of her housecoat.

Suddenly she shivered inside, feeling the touch of his eyes as a physical thing, feeling her breasts swelling into his fingers, feeling his lips plucking at them.

The room seemed to shrink about them, closing in by some weird optical effect that brought him closer without moving. Ruth sucked in her breath, feeling again that panic-flight response, and only too aware that there was nowhere to go.

'I . . . all right,' she agreed, her eyes flicking past him in both directions as she sought some safe route to her bedroom, as she found herself wishing she'd a lock on that bedroom door.

Kurtis merely sat where he was as she skirted her path to the doorway, casting a cautious glance over her shoulder as she turned and plunged towards the bedroom, fleeing as if the very devil was in pursuit.

CHAPTER FOUR

KURTIS slouched in his chair across the restaurant table from Ruth, who was playing with her food, toying with it as she fought for the courage to meet his eyes.

He'd refused to discuss anything—indeed had said hardly a word since she'd emerged from her bedroom in faded jeans and an oversized, baggy sweatshirt, the least flattering outfit she could find.

In his car, she had forced herself hard against the door, almost cringing in her attempt to maintain all possible distance from him. And on entering the restaurant Ruth had been ridiculously pleased to have the waiter hold her chair for her, rather than Kurtis himself.

'We'll talk after we've got some tucker inside us,' was all Kurtis said. 'Hard on the digestion to argue on an empty stomach.'

Now, with a curious look of...determination?...he forced Ruth through sheer force of will to meet his eyes.

'Right, Ruth the witch; you've obviously finished your tea so let's make a start. Do you want to go first, or shall I?'

'It's your party,' she replied. 'I wouldn't even be here, given the choice.' And she flinched inside at the pain which flashed across his eyes. She didn't want to hurt him, and suddenly realised that with a startling intensity. She just couldn't live with him, cope with him, keep up with him.

'OK. Question time. Do you suppose you can manage to tell me, in plain, ordinary language, why you ran away? I think I know—in fact I'm morally sure I do—but I'd like to hear it from you.'

'You ought to know; I left you a note.'

He snorted! 'You left me the sort of note a child writes when he or she's running away from home.'

Fingers rummaged through an inner pocket while he held her with his eyes, forcing her to attend. A piece of paper fluttered across the table to land beside her plate.

'There's your note,' he said, and his voice was alive with anger and frustration. 'Read the damned thing, Ruth. It isn't going to leap up and bite you, although it should. My very oath, it should!'

Ruth plucked up the note with trembling fingers, but she didn't need to read it to know the words. She'd sweated blood at the time just finding those few which had a hope of getting her message across.

It's too much for me. I can't take any more. Please let me go and don't try to find me because it won't do any good.

And Kurtis, it seemed, didn't need the note to know the words either.

'Too much *what*? Couldn't take any more *what*?' he demanded now, and Ruth could tell from his voice that he was very close to erupting. She sat in silence, trying but then failing to meet his eyes, her brain stunned by the fury of his attitude.

'Well? Damn it, Ruth, I'm surely entitled to more than *that*,' he growled.

'I suppose so,' she mused, as much to herself as to him. But then she lapsed into silence again, unable even to think of a place to start. She lowered her head, trying to stem the whirlwind of thought that spun uselessly inside.

'Too fast.' She heard the words—or thought she did—but only just, and looked up to see Kurtis staring into his empty plate. He looked up as if prompted by her own eyes, but gave no sign of having spoken.

She continued to watch him, absorbing the pain she saw within him, wanting to speak but unable to find any adequate words, unsure if she could find them even to explain to herself; she'd tried often enough since leaving him and never truly succeeded.

'I loved you,' she said, and shot upright in her seat at the unexpectedness of *those* words. It wasn't what she'd meant to say at all.

Kurtis stayed silent, but his eyes *willed* her to continue.

'I . . . I just couldn't cope with the lifestyle,' she stammered. 'With the lifestyle and . . . with you.' She stopped, halted by the rising glow in his eyes, by the first hintings of *that* look. Kurtis, as if realising it, bowed his head to stare instead at his plate.

How to explain? How to even begin to explain? Ruth, too, looked down at her plate while she marshalled her thoughts.

'It wasn't so much that you were away so much,' she finally began, knowing this wasn't the way to start, wasn't even the issue. They'd already discussed this, had done so before they married.

'If you married an international cricket player, you'd do it expecting that when you couldn't be with him he'd have to go alone,' Kurtis had said. 'I'm not much different, really. You love your work and don't want to give it up just now, nor should you; it's your career and you're good at it. Of course I'm going to try and restructure my affairs so that I don't have to travel so much, but that will take a lot of time.'

'I understand that,' she had assured him, 'and it won't be a problem; there's no way it should be.'

But it had been! Almost from the very beginning, Ruth had found a vast difference between what she believed and how she really felt about the situation of having a husband who was almost always somewhere else. But that alone hadn't been the problem.

'You're evading the issue,' Kurtis accused her, glaring at her across the table. 'We had that out before we even got married, and I know that, while it was difficult for you at first, you weren't sufficiently upset by that alone to run like you did.'

'You don't know anything,' Ruth retorted. 'And you never will, if you don't give me time to finish.'

Kurtis met her eyes with a frank, steady glance, then bowed and murmured, 'As you wish, my lady witch.' And again, damn him, his eyes started to sing to her.

Ruth looked away, but it was too late. Her entire body started to yield to his song. Her breasts throbbed at the touch of his eyes, their caress at her throat sent her pulse into orbit. She had to forcibly restrain an urge to fidget in her chair because the pit of her stomach had turned to mush.

'We're not getting very far very fast,' he said, but he was speaking to her back as Ruth dashed for the amenities, certain it was her only possible refuge. If she stayed long enough, she prayed, maybe he would give up and leave without her. Then she laughed at her image in the mirror, an almost hysterical laugh at such hysterical thinking.

But as she emerged from the loo the sight of what could only be an emergency exit spurred her to thinking that was even more hysterical. The decision took no courage, much less outright panic. Anything, she thought, was preferable to facing up to her husband in his present mood and her admitted weakness for him.

It was the work of an instant to thrust open the door and peer into the alleyway behind the restaurant, the work of another to step hesitantly into the darkness, then scurry with increasingly long strides to the main street beyond and the chance of a taxi, a bus, anything mobile to assist her flight.

Ruth hit the footpath running, only to come up short as a male figure stepped out, arms spread to catch her as she ran straight into his arms.

Kurtis! She didn't question it, didn't have to. His touch was too familiar, his scent, the very essence of him unquestionable, undeniable. His arms closed around her in an embrace that was more caress than capture, more arousing—deliberately so—than frightening.

Ruth stopped struggling almost as soon as she began, her body replying to his embrace while her mind screamed silently against it. Strong fingers gripped her shoulders with such gentleness that she should have easily been able to free herself, yet somehow couldn't. Warm breath touched at her cheek, her ear, as his words insinuated themselves into her consciousness.

'You're only fooling yourself, you know. You're trying to run from yourself, Ruth, and you can't—Any more than you can run from me now. Your running's over and your coffee's waiting, so make up your mind if you want to come quietly or be carried.'

'Let me go.'

Ruth said the words, but they emerged as neither a plea nor a demand, merely a whispered emptiness to the night air. She slumped in his arms, defeated by the feel of his body against her, defeated by how easily he'd managed to stay one step ahead of her all the way.

'Shall we go home instead of having coffee?' he asked, ignoring her words, keeping her close against him, trapped in his arms and surely just as trapped by her own emotions, by her own fears.

'No,' she replied, then repeated herself. 'No. Let's have coffee, please.'

Coffee, tea, milk, another meal, anything... anything but a return to her tiny flat where she would have to be alone with him again, defenceless against whatever weapons he chose to use.

Ruth returned to the restaurant, her eyes downcast, certain everybody in the place must be looking at her, must *know* of her futile flight, her obvious capture. Kurtis, striding easily beside her, seemed oblivious to the possibility of any embarrassment. He would be, she thought. It was typical of him simply to ignore such a possibility.

As they approached the table, their cooling coffee was replaced by fresh, but it was far less simple to replace Ruth's feeling of despair at the entire situation.

And Kurtis knew it! He took his place across from her, calmly stirring his coffee as he sought her with his eyes, using them to reach out and touch her, to caress her, to fondle her. His voice he used as a weapon.

'Are you going to try and keep avoiding this forever, Ruth?' he asked, voice low but sufficient to carry across the sudden intimacy of the setting.

'I'm not trying to avoid anything,' she insisted, lying, knowing it, knowing he knew it as well. 'I didn't ask you to come; I didn't ask you to... to...'

'To try and save my marriage—*our* marriage—while there's still time? No, you didn't. But you should have, judging from the way you're acting,' he replied.

'It's over.'

'It is not over.' And now his eyes fairly blazed. 'It's not over until we *make* it be over, and that, dear lady witch, we have yet to do.'

'Don't call me that!' Ruth shuddered even as she snarled at him, shuddered at how those few words could so easily stab her like a knife, could so easily demoralise her.

'You used to like it,' he remarked quietly, not really arguing with her, but making his point none the less.

'It used to mean something,' Ruth replied coldly.

'It still does,' Kurtis said, his eyes as cold as her words.

'Maybe to you,' she sneered, but kept her eyes averted. She couldn't say that and meet his gaze. And he knew it, she realised.

Fingers cupped at her chin, lightly lifting her head so that she had to meet his eyes.

'To you, too, and there's no sense denying it, Ruth, any more than there's any sense in trying to deny that you loved me, and still do.'

'Which means nothing, especially to you,' she replied. 'If it ever did, which I doubt.'

'That's a bit heavy, don't you think? After all, you have it in writing, and many times over, if I may say so.'

'Me and how many other girls?' she snapped, reality now creeping in to put a firm texture to her pain. 'I bet there are thousands of your so-called love letters floating around, tucked away in bureau drawers, buried in a thousand glory boxes.'

The fury of the challenge seemed to miss him; he sat and regarded her soberly, his eyes soft now with feelings or memory, his voice when he spoke equally soft.

'And where do you keep yours?' he suddenly asked.

'Under the kitchen sink with the rest of the rubbish,' she cried, lying and knowing he knew she was lying, knowing herself it was a smaller lie than she'd intended, that she'd really wanted to tell him she hadn't bothered to keep his letters, not daring to admit she couldn't even imagine *not* keeping them.

Ruth could feel the tears gathering behind her eyes, could feel the hot coals of frustration building inside her tummy. How dared he come back into her life *now*? How dared he dredge up the feelings and emotions she'd so carefully buried? It wasn't fair, she wanted to cry, but she didn't, because that, too, would be an admission of how strong her feelings remained.

'Every word of every letter I ever wrote you was the simple truth,' he said, and his voice dared her to deny it, even to try to deny it. 'Every word!'

'At the time, perhaps,' Ruth grudgingly admitted, although it really wasn't an admission so much as a fruitless try to make him shut up, to make him change the subject.

'I don't recall putting a time limit on anything,' he said then, and she could have screamed with the frustration of it all. She didn't want this discussion, didn't want him there, sitting across from her, able to touch her with his eyes, with his very presence.

'And especially not on your so-called "trapline",' Ruth replied, and could have bitten off her tongue. It wasn't what she had intended to say, wasn't what she'd wanted to say. She couldn't even begin to imagine where the words had come from!

Kurtis raised one eyebrow and his mouth quirked into a semblance of a grin, but it was a grin without humour, chilling in its coldness.

'Ah,' he sighed, then fell silent. But the single exhalation was enough to drag Ruth back into memory, back into the wonder of his letters, his weird, convoluted mind, his inane sense of humour. And one letter, especially, which had arrived about a week after his second visit to Hobart, after he had taken Ruth to her own bed in an explosion of emotions and sheer physical delight that she never would, never could, forget.

In the letter Kurtis had used, as he occasionally did, an alter-ego servant to put into words what he apparently felt uncomfortable about saying for himself.

You, my lady witch admit not planning for romance on this year's agenda. My master, lusty fellow that he is, did, of course, plan on it—but only in terms of casual dalliance. His trapline—about which more later—was set with quick-release equipment. A good workman never blames his tools, so my master suspects he, himself, has lost his touch. Or else, he wonders, has he strayed too far afield and wandered into a witchly snare, forgotten and unnoticed? Or, most likely, a bit of both and isn't it bloody wonderful? Sorry, my mistress, I was carried away by the magic of it all. Is it not truly amazing, however, how the best laid plans...etc? And even more wonderful how impossible it is to release something that is already free, and cherished for it?

Kurtis's 'trapline' was something they'd discussed more or less as a joke, he insisting it was so little used as to be irrelevant, Ruth not particularly concerned one way or the other until their going to bed together had made it exceptionally relevant—at least in her own eyes.

The exquisite Rosemary had emerged then, as if in some rude parody of their private witch-warlock personalities, and hovered spectre-like over Ruth's feelings about Kurtis and their entire relationship.

She had therefore been of two minds when confronted with the way his letter continued.

My master bids me to report that the aforementioned trapline has fallen into such general disuse as to be abandoned. Except, of course, for the Hobart spur! The trap in the herb garden, unfortunately, has a release mechanism tangled with a certain amount of undischarged obligation, and, lest innocent plants be injured in the untangling, my master begs your indulgence, faith, and understanding in this matter. This is all, of course, his own fault for not sticking to the agenda, but dear my mistress, he does have a conscience, truly he does...

Ruth had read those passages so often she knew them by heart almost a year later, and still they had the power both to quicken her heart and stab it with icicles at the same time.

At the time it had been easy enough, her romance so buoyant, so all-encompassing that understanding of a sort had come easily, almost willingly.

Of course Kurtis had been involved with Rosemary, and of course there were 'undischarged obligations'; they were, after all, linked in business together. He had never admitted nor even suggested a physical involvement, and Ruth knew that at the time she had never truly considered one. Had never wanted to, had shrugged off as much as she could the elegant woman's insinuations in that direction. Now, of course, she could see that as selective seeing and hearing; there *had* been a physical involvement and only a love-struck fool could have missed it!

Only a love-struck fool, only a woman obsessed with love for its own sake, could have so blithely ignored Rosemary's needling remarks, could have ignored the woman's possessive attitude, her haughty, self-assured smugness.

But I was in love, gullible, naïve—especially naïve—and I got exactly what I asked for, Ruth now thought, looking at Kurtis across the restaurant table but not really seeing him. What she was seeing was herself, those many months ago, when he'd followed up that particular letter some weeks later with a gesture so typically flamboyant, so totally outrageous, that it had knocked her flat. Just as he'd intended, the devious, cunning swine that he was!

The parcel had arrived without a return address, without a note inside, without a single word of explanation. Not that it had needed any, really. Or so she'd thought upon opening it to stare with initial bewilderment at the contents.

Tidily packed in an audio cassette's plastic case, sealed with a stick-on heart, had been a mousetrap with a sprig of green plant caught under the killing bar.

Ruth had stood staring at it, bemused, for some moments before the message fairly leapt out at her. The sprig of green was rosemary, and what Kurtis had sent her was, if his convoluted logic meant anything at all, the trap from the herb garden!

She had laughed then, only to find her laughter waning to tears of relief at the unlikely token and at just how really significant it was, tears of joy and wonder that he would recognise her needs, would bother to pander to them.

It couldn't be clearer, she'd thought at the time. He'd abandoned his trapline, just as the earlier letter had promised, and this was the final trap, the one clogged with what he'd so tidily called, through his servant, 'undischarged obligations'. It was probably what Kurtis occasionally referred to as a 'definitive statement', she'd thought at the time. And had been pleased to accept that definition, delighted to accept it.

Her relief must have been obvious when he'd telephoned a few days later and casually, late in the conversation, had asked if she'd received 'the parcel'.

'Yes,' she'd replied.

'No problem understanding it?'

'No,' she'd said, only to wonder if the parcel had contained some *other* message, some more subtle message that she somehow might have missed.

She had rushed to extricate it from where it lived, with every letter he'd written, in the drawer of her bedside table, and had examined the box from every possible angle without learning anything new. It was, quite obviously, the trap from the herb garden, Kurtis's definitive statement that Rosemary was no longer an issue. If there were any other message involved, she'd have to wait for him to explain it.

Which he never had, although not for lack of opportunity, and it wasn't until after they were married and it was too late that Ruth had realised why!

But another tribute to her innocence, her sheer *naïveté*, she thought now. If Kurtis himself had given her no startling clues to what was *really* going on, Rosemary herself had provided a multitude, each typical of her devious sophistication.

'It was all a lie, wasn't it?' Ruth asked, making the question an accusation, her voice icy, her bluntness deliberate.

Enough of this, she suddenly thought. If he wanted meaningful dialogue, he'd damned well get it. Perhaps *then* he would leave her alone, get out of her life once and for all, leave her to go on in her own way, without him, without his damnable letters, his damnable ability to turn her on and off like a light switch.

'What was all a lie?'

'You had…Rosemary in your bed before you met me, and she never really left it, did she? She was always there, even after…after we were…were married.' Ruth had to struggle to get the words out, found Rosemary's very name seemed to cloy on her lips, found the thought of Kurtis and Rosemary together just as sick-making as it had, almost a year ago, when she'd left him.

Kurtis didn't reply immediately. He stared across the table at her, glanced down at his coffee, then up to meet Ruth's eyes once again. His own eyes were unreadable, merely pools of bleak emptiness.

Then he shook his head, sadly, and finally said, 'You really believe that. Which makes it an impossible accusation to refute, because I can see that you're not going to believe me no matter what I say.'

'Probably.' Ruth's voice was as bleak as his eyes, deliberately.

'And is that what all this is about?' he asked in a voice so low she could barely hear him. 'Is that why you left, why you ran, why we've spent the past near as dammit a year apart? Just *that*?'

'*Just* that? I would have thought it was more than enough,' Ruth replied hotly. Although it wasn't *just* that. That was only a tiny portion of what had gone wrong, had been wrong from the very start, if she'd only had the sense to realise it, Ruth knew. And even now the problem was putting it into words, because that would mean admitting her own flaws.

It would mean admitting that her own lack of self-worth, her own sense of inadequacy, her lack of sophistication and her lack of confidence had all been contributing factors. That because she couldn't feel comfortable in Kurtis's high-flying lifestyle she had run from it—and from him. Rosemary was only an excuse and Ruth knew it; knew she could have forgiven him Rosemary, but she couldn't forgive herself for not being able to compete, for never really trying.

'It would be enough if it were true, I suppose,' Kurtis mused, not bothering to meet her eyes. He wasn't trying to fight her accusation, didn't seem much fussed about it all. 'It might even be enough if that were all there was to it, which we both know it isn't,' he continued, now gazing sombrely at her but without even the heat of anger in his eyes, just a placid calm that was somehow more disturbing.

'I know what *I* know,' Ruth retorted. 'What *you* know, or think you know, isn't my concern any more.'

'Want to bet?' And now his eyes flashed with…something. It didn't appear to be anger, although Ruth couldn't be totally sure. Kurtis was slow to anger, she knew, and during the length of their relationship she had hardly ever seen him truly angry. And never, she realised, truly angry with *her*!

'Anyway,' he said abruptly, 'this isn't getting us anywhere; I don't know why I should have thought it would.'

And, rising to his feet, he stalked across to the cashier without a backward glance, paid the bill, then shot an impatient look at Ruth and walked over to the exit, where he stood waiting until she joined him.

Once on the footpath, he walked swiftly to where the car was parked, while she, with little alternative, could only follow at her own pace. He drove back to her flat in silence, but it was too much to hope that he would simply drop her off and leave—oh, no! He was right there with her when Ruth unlocked the door, had followed her in before she had any chance to object, and seconds later was ensconced on her lounge suite, his eyes directing her to sit in her habitual chair.

'We've had enough coffee for now, I think,' he said gravely. 'But not enough of what is euphemistically termed "meaningful dialogue". Ignoring, for now, this rubbish about Rosemary and me, what other things contributed to the downfall of our marriage, Ruth?'

And then, to her horror, he clammed up. He sat there, silent and disapproving, his presence seeming to fill the room like a giant black cloud, demanding answers, demanding that she respond. They sat staring at each other for what seemed hours, Ruth determined not to be dominated, Kurtis so totally at ease that he dominated without any effort at all. Ruth broke first.

'I don't see why we should *ignore* the issue of you and Rosemary,' she began, only to have him wave her comment aside with a swipe of his hand, a contemptuous wave.

'Stop being evasive,' he growled. 'It's a load of rubbish and you either know it or you should.' And then, with frightening insight, 'Besides, if that's the best argument you can present for having run like a rabbit, I'm wasting my time even being here because my judgement is so totally questionable as to have no value at all.'

His eyes glowed now, his gaze roving over Ruth with a casual familiarity that fairly screamed out possession, intimate knowledge. 'And my judgement was *never* that bad,' he said, his voice soft-edged but firm as cement.

'Maybe,' Ruth heard herself replying in a voice she could barely recognise, 'that's been the problem all along. Maybe your judgement of me has always been totally questionable.'

His snort of derision was as explosive as the movement which suddenly had him before her, his hands clasping her upper arms to lift her to her feet, forcing her to face him from inches away.

'Hmmph!' he snorted. And his mouth then swooped down to capture her lips, his kiss punishing, a fearful blend of hot and cold, gentle and rough, seeking and demanding.

Ruth had no chance to avoid the kiss, no chance once begun really to fight against it. His lips forced her to respond; his closeness was a ruthless assault on her personal space, her determination not to let him touch her.

The kiss went on and on and on, his grip on her arms holding her still while his mouth plundered her own, his breath sweetly mingling with hers despite her objections. Never in all their relationship had he kissed her with impersonal and yet intimate effect; never had he used physical means with such strength, such anger.

But then, as abruptly as he'd begun it, he stopped. Ruth was quite unceremoniously released, to land with a thud back in her chair. The impact was sufficient to blur her vision, and when it returned she saw Kurtis back in his own seat, glaring at her with what could have been hostility or just plain satisfaction.

'Right...enough of the bulldust,' he growled. 'You have the floor, my lady witch, and I would advise you to make the most of it, because otherwise we're going to be at this for a very, very long time.'

Ruth could only stare, her mind a kaleidoscope of images, her emotional state so thoroughly confused, she hardly knew what she felt. Even her anger had been disrupted; she now felt only a kind of disorientation.

Kurtis remained silent, watching her with the patience of some great predator, his eyes revealing nothing, his posture showing only a readiness to get physical again if such were needed.

Ruth dropped her eyes, fighting for control, struggling to find some order to her thoughts. But Kurtis grew impatient with her delaying tactics, and spoke before she could.

'Let's start with the premise, dear Ruth, that our whole relationship went too fast for you right from the beginning, which is my fault in a way, although before God I did *try* to keep the speed down to something manageable. Obviously, I failed, or is that putting it just too simply for you?'

'It...yes, it was too fast,' she finally managed to say. But that wasn't a sufficient explanation and she knew it. 'But...it wasn't really your fault; it was mine more than anyone's.'

How it hurt to utter those words, yet how great the relief actually to say it out loud! Ruth sighed with the relief, sighed with having taken that undeniable fact out and laid it between them, finally visible for what it was.

Kurtis sighed too, but his sigh was one of anger, of rank frustration.

'I should have known,' he muttered softly. 'I asked you often enough, and even though you always denied it the fact that I was prompted to ask should have warned me.'

Ruth was silent. So much she could have said, perhaps should have said, but too late now. Too late, she thought, to admit that Kurtis had, quite literally, swept her off her feet; that his letters, his attitudes, his very being had created such a whirlwind of romance that she'd been lifted beyond logic, beyond reality—only to come to earth with an almighty thud when the dream had been brought to an end.

'Aren't you going to say anything, Ruth?' His voice was strangely soft now, his attitude also softened as he leaned back in his chair to sit watching her.

'There...there isn't much to say,' she replied. 'It was too fast, certainly. I was too...naïve, I guess, to realise where fantasy ended—*must* end—and reality began. Too naïve, too young, too unsophisticated—certainly that. And far, far too gullible to see the whole thing for what it was!'

The last few words escaped with a hiss of bitterness that surprised even Ruth. Kurtis certainly caught it; his eyebrow rose and his eyes hardened noticeably.

'What it was? And just exactly what was that, Ruth?'

'You know all too well,' she snapped, not wanting to be drawn further but knowing it was now inevitable.

'If I knew it all too well, I wouldn't have to be here,' he replied in a too calm voice. 'So tell me—just how did I play upon this so-called gullibility?'

Ruth paused before answering, gathering strength, fighting the fickleness of her upset tummy, her shortness of breath. And when she did reply, it all came out in a burst of anger and hurt that she couldn't stop, didn't want to stop.

'I was always just a joke to you, and to your friends,' she charged. 'The so-called witch, the innocent, naïve country girl, the Tasmanian—maybe not with two heads, but just as laughable for all that. A joke...that's what I was. A cruel, hateful, nasty joke.'

Kurtis made to speak, but Ruth shushed him angrily, shouting now, as she raged through a litany of the abuses she'd suffered during their brief period of togetherness— the sniggers of his friends, the downright rudeness, the way she'd been subjected to a constant barrage of criticism and laughter over her hair, her clothing, her lack of sophistication. Then she launched into the innuendo, the passes she'd had to fend off from social contacts who, she insisted, should have known better; the way she was certain—but could never prove—that his precious damned Rosemary had been the driving force behind it all; the way it had hurt, *still* hurt...

And in the end she sat, huddled in her chair, arms clasped about her middle and her head bowed in exhaustion—but not in defeat, not in blind acceptance. Never again that!

And Kurtis sat, silent, until she finally looked up at him and threw out her final, most cutting accusation.

'You people have the morals of alley-cats,' she sneered. 'There isn't enough honesty in the lot of you to produce one iota of real affection, real love, real...real anything! And you can all go to blazes for all I care, because I'm *me* and I'm damned if I'll be ashamed of that! Unsophisticated, naïve, whatever...I'm *me*.'

And once again she lowered her head, willing him to give it up now, just to get up and leave and never come back.

But when he did finally speak, his words gave no indication he had any such plans; quite the opposite, in fact.

'I'm glad you got that lot of rubbish out in the open,' he said, and she looked up to see that he was sitting with his eyes closed, as if pondering on every word.

'It's not *rubbish*, except, I suppose, to you,' she replied, her bitterness still a foul taste in her mouth.

'It's rubbish to both of us,' he said bluntly. 'And now its out where we can actually talk about it, I think—I hope—that maybe I can make you see that. Damn it, Ruth, are you so bitter, so blind, that you can't see that your so-called unsophistication is one of the things I love *best* about you? Can't you see that I love you for what you *are*, not for what other people might see, or not see, or...whatever? What do you think all those love letters were saying, anyway? I didn't write them just for my health, you know.'

And before Ruth could even begin to reply he rose to his feet and stood, glaring down at her like some medieval inquisitor, his eyes fairly blazing, his fingers knotting into fists that kept flexing and unflexing.

'I will admit to a lot of things,' he said. 'I didn't realise how difficult it was going to be to reorganise business matters so we could spend sufficient time together, I didn't take enough account of just how much too fast I was pushing you into a relationship you obviously weren't ready for, and I certainly didn't allow for the influence of other people—because those other people weren't important, their opinions weren't important and I never for one minute guessed you'd ever consider them important.

'But I never, *never* laughed at you, Ruth. You were never a joke to me, not then and not now. And I've never, never ever been ashamed of you, or embarrassed by you, or any of this other rubbish you've been mouthing off about. I can hardly credit any of it! It just doesn't make any sense to me at all.'

And then, abruptly, he turned and strode angrily towards the doorway, turning finally to stand in it, scowling, quite obviously furious.

'I'm going now, before I say something I might end up being sorry for,' he said, and his voice was ice, colder than ice. 'But don't think this is over, because it isn't and it never damned well will be. Not like this. Damn it!' he snarled, and thumped the doorframe with his fist in a gesture so angry, so vivid with frustration that Ruth found herself flinching despite the distance between them. 'Damn it!' he said again, and his eyes burned across the room. 'I must have time to think about this, Ruth. I'll go now, and come again in the morning after I've had a chance to try and make some sense of it all—if that's possible. I just can't imagine you throwing away what we had on the basis of what *other* people might have said, or done, or thought.

'I didn't marry you for other people. I married you for *me*, for *us*. Anybody else—everybody else—had nothing to do with it, and I just can't see for the life of me why you would ever have thought otherwise.'

Then, to her astonishment, he shrugged, throwing off his angry expression to replace it with a rueful grin.

'Maybe, my love, it's time you hauled out all those letters and read them again, only this time try reading between the lines as well, because they weren't as frivolous as they might have seemed. You seem to have forgotten that. Those letters are *me*, Ruth, and what they say about my feelings for you is more than just a bunch of pretty words. You *read* them, and then I *dare* you to say that I've laughed at you or belittled you or patronised you. *Ever*! I may be guilty of a lot of things, but never that.

'*Read* them, Ruth, and in the morning we'll try and talk about this whole damned thing sensibly, like adults,' he said. 'And while you're at it, try remembering that I love you, because I do. No matter what else, I do love you and I believe you love me, too.'

He turned away, then turned back abruptly to catch her with his gaze, holding her like a sheepdog facing up to a stubborn ewe.

'No more running, Ruth,' he said in a curiously gentle tone—and was suddenly gone, leaving her in a silence broken only by the sound of the outside door closing behind him.

Ruth sat, eyes closed and mind buffeted by whirlwinds of emotion and scattered thoughts, oblivious to the tears she could feel leaking from her eyes. She felt exhausted; her very bones ached from the tension, her head felt stuffed with cotton wool. Moving as if in a trance, she stumbled about the flat, tidying up the coffee-cups, turning out lights, getting ready for bed. Trying, throughout, to make some sense out of all Kurtis had said, all that she had felt, had wanted to say and didn't, hadn't.

Read his letters? Again? How many times did he think she must read them? she wondered. They were already burned into her memory; she could have recited them almost word for word, had he demanded it.

She went to bed in the dark, determined simply to sleep and rebuild her strength, to think of nothing... Only to find his face alive in her mind, his presence like a ghost in the bed beside her.

Her skin seemed to tingle, feeling in memory his touch, his warmth. Then she shivered, fighting for the strength that had let her leave him, the determination that had carried her through the past months without him.

Damn him, she thought. Damn and double damn! Just when she thought herself cured of him, just when she thought her life was back under control—*her* control— he could just walk in and fill an emptiness she had been sure didn't even exist. To hell with him, and to hell with his letters.

And then she found herself reaching for the bedside lamp, opening the drawer and taking out the letters, hating herself as she did so but unable to resist. He wanted her to read them again...she would. But reading them wouldn't change anything, she thought. Reading them wouldn't change the fact that, no matter what he *said* he didn't love her and never really had. It had all been just a cruel game to him, a casual dalliance with literary pretensions.

Ruth sneered at herself for bothering, cursed Kurtis roundly as she started with his very first letter, and found herself still reading, all thought of sleep long departed, several hours later.

CHAPTER FIVE

'DEAR my lady witch...' Each and every letter began so, in what had become, to Ruth, almost a secret language, a magical language of love and wonderment and, now, hurt and confusion.

Dawn was painting the horizon a galah-belly pink while she was still reading Kurtis's letters, her eyes tired and grainy, her mind twitching from the effort, her heart saddened by it all. She realised now that, despite actually memorising entire sections of the letters, despite having read each of them individually until the ink had nearly worn away, she had never really read them in sequence, never tried to link their thoughts, their messages, *his* thinking.

And just as well, she thought, or she might well have crumpled beneath the strain. Still might, because, exhausted as she was from the reading and the evening before, she couldn't, with any honesty, avoid facing up to what the damned letters *really* said.

Kurtis had been right when he said the letters were *him*, that they said everything he'd ever tried to say to her. Using his warlock persona and that of the faithful servant type, and even occasionally writing in his own voice, he had done his level best to try and communicate with Ruth as fully and as effectively as he could.

To which she, in turn, had replied with brief, frivolous notes of her own, not trusting her own powers of written communication to relay her true feelings, and never—she realised now—giving the letters the answers they deserved at the time.

'I read into the things what I wanted to hear,' she muttered at one point, unaware she was speaking aloud until her own voice startled her, even less inclined to admit even in the slightest just how much more there was to the letters when they were taken in context and sequence.

The saga of a love-affair, they were, or at least of half a love-affair. Throughout, there was a common thread, one of caring, of concern, of Kurtis opening himself up in total vulnerability, knowing his own flaws and faults, trying to let Ruth know them, too, trying to protect her from ... himself? Or from her own *naïveté*, her inability to look seriously, critically, at what he knew from his greater experience *had* to be looked at seriously sooner or later?

And they also, without contradiction, maintained his abiding fear that he was pushing Ruth too fast into the intimacy of their relationship, that he was giving her neither time nor room to come to terms with it as she would.

Almost from the beginning he had done so; the words of his so-called servant fairly leapt from one page at Ruth, words she had read and reread perhaps a dozen times before, but never quite taken in...

And finally, bewilderingly to me, my illustrious master bids me note his concern that some elements of his last—yesterday's—missive might lead your exemplary self to believe that your wondrous love-affair might somehow be going too fast for your elegant tastes. Considering how long it took him to compose that epistle, even with my dynamic help, the logic of this concern totally escapes my humble self, but perhaps your exalted wisdom can make sense of it.

Should this astonishing situation actually exist, I am directed to inform your eminence that my master would, purely out of love and admiration for you, cease and desist at your order. Immediately, if not sooner, provided you operated appropriately upon his fingernails with a pair of pliers. But he wouldn't like it, I can assure your magnificence, and would probably do something quite drastic. It is surely a source of great concern to your splendid personage that a rampant chauvinist, a lusty conqueror of fair witch-maidens like my esteemed master would even *consider* such wimpy thoughts. It may be that he is simply trying to stir, a bit, though the folly of such bravado clearly indicates an unstable mind. Would a sane warlock chance his luck against your thunderbolts, dare to stick his magic wand into your personal cauldron, so to speak?

And when he was being serious, Kurtis could be extremely so. With the questionable benefit of hindsight, Ruth reread one segment and wondered if the sheer intensity of it hadn't caused her to put it aside, ignore the depth of feeling it now seemed to portray...

Together, we could go where neither of us has ever been before. Dare I suggest, my most loved mistress lady witch, that we already have? And the adventure has scarce begun! We could find paradise together, you and I. But, the gods being ever fickle, we also may have to go through hell together at some time or another. I'd rather go to hell by myself, but I can't find paradise alone.

Ignore it? Yes, she thought. At the time it had been too, too intense, too powerful. And later—because surely she would have read it again—she had read all the letters, or at least most, while coming to the decision to leave her hollow marriage—later she had...she must have missed that one, she decided——

Only to run across Kurtis quoting *her*, taking one of her rare serious replies to his romantic campaign and once again broaching the issue of moving too fast for her comfort...

'Please, I've enjoyed your company but my strength comes to me when my back is against a wall, not when I'm loved. I'm vulnerable too,' she had written. Or so he had said, replying through his servant.

A plea from the heart, my mistress! No wonder my master hath taken to his bed; clearly his thoughts about going too fast were well-founded, and he is distraught. But lo, he creaks geriatrically to his feet, calling out in his anguish. A lover's strength, he says, is the strength of ten; a warlock lover's, the strength of twenty. Besides, right now you're standing in a doorway with the wall hopefully far behind you. Look outward, upward, not back. The wall isn't going anywhere.

Ruth had only the vaguest memory of having written what he said she had, even less memory of ever absorbing the plea linked with his response.

'Because I didn't want to?' she asked herself aloud, and wondered how she could have been so selective in her reading, how she could have failed to see the seriousness, the sheer, vivid intensity that now seemed to leap from his frivolous style.

And yet, she *had* tried, or at least it seemed she had. Once again her selective memory failed her in recalling having written exactly what Kurtis had said she wrote...

'How does one write letters of a romantic nature when even witches haven't ever done it before...?' My master—whose eyes are beginning to fail him as the paper wears thin—and I for once agree: *perfectly*! My master, who as you know is wont to try and hide his feelings in verbosity—usually failing because your witchly eye is sharper than his warlock mind—is actually quite envious. And honoured beyond words, needless to say. Deeply honoured, and moved almost to tears!

Ruth, too, was almost moved to tears, but her tears now were more of frustration and exhaustion than anything else. Kurtis had wrapped his concerns in verbosity and flowery language, but she had totally concealed her own in silence. Nowhere ever, she realised, had she told him of her own concerns, of how she felt so gauche, so naïve, so...*country* that she was ill at ease with his business associates, overwhelmed by the speed and expense of their married lifestyle, inadequate to the role she thought he expected her to fill. Or had he? Nowhere in these letters was there a word about that!

It was full daylight now. Kurtis would be showing up...almost at any moment or as late as lunchtime? He hadn't really said. And as she read on, and on, so much of his writing began to prey upon her conscience, if not that of his alter-ego servant...

Of course your esteemed self will realise that my master would have tossed out his rusty, antiquated traps some time ago—well, last month, anyway—if he'd had the sense God gave a brown dog. Certainly I, his very conscience, told him to do so, but I am but a meek and humble servant. His newly released ego, after years of captivity, positively *demanded* a sop or two, and my master foolishly allowed it over my objections. To his great shame.

However, be not concerned. In the confusion—pandemonium—which followed the arrival of your most powerful spell, when, as you doubtless remember, my master was prostrate and certainly not his normal lusty self, I was able, in darkest secret—the master still doesn't know, for sure—to lure that fickle ego into the dungeon's foulest, darkest cell. And there he shall stay, oh, my mistress, on a diet of vegetables, until he learns a bit of humility! Of course, there may be a price for this, but we are reasonable folk, are we not?

Now, mistress, having established our credentials, as it were, may I comment freely upon your last missive? Of course I may, and shall. You make mention of a certain chain reaction of music . . . surely an apt choice of words. My master has, with my help of course, been seeking a similar description for the effect you have on him. And his, while of course more flowery and wordy, had evolved to "Something in her sings to me" by the time your letter arrived to set him straight. Amazing, is it not, how great minds think alike and weak ones seldom differ?

One weak mind, at the very least, she thought, and got up to make yet another coffee and peer out of the window. It would be just like Kurtis to arrive this early, she thought, then shivered inwardly at memories of the joyous dawns they'd shared, dawns when he was home and the sharing was too exciting, too purely exhilarating for both of them and they had found they simply *had* to get up, to *do* something, even if it was no more than go for a walk.

Gulping at the steaming brew, Ruth read on, her heart lurching at various poignant phrases, her body restless now, becoming attuned to Kurtis's words, his message. She squirmed in her chair, wanting to get the task over with, but unable to keep herself from loitering over some of what he'd said...

I can't promise never to hurt you, because I try never to make promises I can't be sure of keeping, and, because I'm only a man with human failings, I probably will hurt you some day in some fashion, however unintentionally. I can't promise never to leave you, for much the same reasons. I *can* promise to do my best for you and for me and for us, and I do so. I *can* promise to love you as well as I can for as long as I can or as long as you'll let me. And I do so. The logistics problems are quite irrelevant; we can sort out *anything* and we've got the rest of our lives to do it in, together.

I miss you, I feel incomplete without you, because whenever we are together I'm aware of how we complement each other in terms of emotions and feelings and attitudes. I'm just so comfortable with you; I hardly know you and yet I *know* you, for what sense that makes. Know you and like you and love you and cherish you, as witch and woman.

There was one remark my *servant* made that—miraculously—said exactly what it was meant to say, and thus bears repeating: 'He wishes only to be the best person that he *can* be as he grows to become the best person he *could* be, and to find favour in your sight.' That'll do me.

Damn your servant, Ruth thought, inwardly cringing at the thought but unable to ignore it. Damn the master and the man, because she dared not do otherwise! Some of their writings were just too close to the bone for comfort, touched her in ways she had thought herself now immune to...

Well, it's early Thursday morning now, and I've spent a restless night thinking of everything I forgot to include in the letter I finished about two a.m. So much I want to say, so much I'm not sure how to say, not enough paper in the world anyway.

I love you. I cherish you. I need you. I respect you. I care for you. I want you. I want you with me. I want to share my life with you. I have to believe you feel the same way because otherwise I'm wasting my time writing this, although even that couldn't stop me doing so.

Before the day's out, you may get a phone call demanding in the nicest possible terms, of course—that you go through your files and read all my letters in order, starting with the two intense ones that knocked you flat. I think you should; I wish you would. I haven't, although tempted, because I *know* they'll show the consistency of my feelings and my thoughts.

Why hadn't she? Ruth could only sit and stare at those few paragraphs, her mind a whirl and yet blank, as if it were stuck in a snowstorm. It was—had been—a simple enough request. But she hadn't done it, *knew* she hadn't. But she couldn't for the life of her understand why. Especially considering some of the stuff that followed...

I'm afraid that I'm pushing you too fast in this whole thing, or to be more correct I think we're pushing each other too fast. But I don't know how to slow down and I doubt you do either.

I'm not being chauvinistic, Ruth, or if I am I don't care because it has to be said. You're a good woman, a fine woman, a woman with guts and a woman to be proud of. But you're a loving, caring, delightful, flighty woman who needs a man to love and care for and who can take delight in you and love you for all that you are. And you know it! And I'm that man and you know that, too.

I don't want to see you old and alone; I want you old with me! If it's what *you* want.

I have to stop this or I'll be on your doorstep this afternoon, which wouldn't help anything. Just please, Ruth, *don't run*! I know you're tempted and I know why. We can cool it if you want to, if you have to; we can stop dead in our tracks if it helps, but just please don't run. Don't quit. Don't give up just because you're scared.

Scared? I should have been terrified, Ruth thought. I should have been running like a rabbit, just as I finally did do. But even more, she realised with the wonder of hindsight, she should have been somehow responding to Kurtis's concerns, should have been communicating with him as he had so obviously been trying to communicate with her. She should have—but she hadn't! She had instead concealed her worries, kept her concerns from him, hidden them even from herself, where she could. They were too *real*, too much a part of her she hadn't wanted to face at the time, still didn't. Too far from the magic, too real to fit in her concepts of romance.

It wasn't as if they couldn't talk to each other; when they were together—both before the wedding and afterwards—one of the nicest things had been their aptitude of companionable talk. But, she realised with a flash of insight, those times had never lent themselves to the sort of serious, intense discussion Kurtis must have sensed was required.

He had tried; these letters revealed how hard he'd tried. But *she* hadn't. She hadn't tried at all, had found it all too easy to throw her worries aside, to ignore the problems, ignore the feelings that had eventually built up to the explosion that made her run.

A passage in yet another letter caught her eye, and she read it thrice over because somehow, now, it seemed so apt...

It seems every time we start talking seriously you take your flighty little dance closer and closer to the precipice, only to find some tricky little pirouette that rescues you just as you're about to tip over and fall for my warlock's charms. Very frustrating, it is, especially when all I want is for you to admit we *might* have a future and that you *want* us to have a future and we *both* want it to be a long and fulfilling future—together. However unconventionally in the short term!

But I'm a patient type, even if it mightn't seem so. I shall addict you to my loving, to my touch, to my caring and sharing and to the person that I am, which is the right person for you just as you're the right woman for me. And once I have you addicted—as I am—it'll be maintenance rations—with just the occasional flare-up to keep things interesting—to make sure I have enough reserves to last the distance. So be warned, this is a long-term campaign you're being threatened with.

'Be warned'! Well, she had been. And had ignored the warning in ways that now seemed terribly important, even more terrible in the way she felt uncomfortable, almost ashamed at how she'd failed to see the letters for the seriousness that was in them.

Ruth continued to work her way through the stack, finding them less intense, increasingly so in the days leading up to their wedding, and almost all the intensity gone in those she'd received afterwards, from a husband more often away than home. The later letters were more frivolous, far lighter, clearly designed to entertain, not to raise serious doubts or provoke serious discussions.

It was almost as if, having got her to the altar, Kurtis had decided she must have known what she was doing and chosen to accept that. As she had, until the pent-up, unrelieved cauldron of emotion inside her had finally boiled over.

Until she had, as he said, run like a rabbit.

Suddenly, unbidden, his voice seemed to come into her mind, and she could hear him explaining what must be done if they were going to have, as he put it, a 'more or less conventional relationship'.

He was, he had explained, like a juggler with a thousand pretty glass balls in the air. One slip could bring the whole lot smashing to the ground, but sufficient fancy footwork and a very, very careful attitude would allow him to reduce the number slowly until he ended up with a tidy, manageable business structure that would allow him to work from Hobart—or wherever they might choose—without the incessant travel and insane hours he'd been working when they met.

'It will take the best part of a year, maybe longer,' he'd said, launching into rafts of detail Ruth couldn't understand, didn't particularly want to, and really didn't think she needed to. If that was what Kurtis said, it would be all right, she'd thought. But it hadn't been.

He had spent far more time away from her during that ten months of marriage than he'd spent with her. Had it not been for her work, things might have been different—certainly he had encouraged her to go with him whenever it was possible. But she had *loved* her work, had retained her concepts of a nursing *career*, even through the headiest days of their romance. And he had agreed. She liked Hobart, loved living in Tasmania despite an admitted lack of knowledge about other places. Kurtis, with his worldly experience, also loved Tasmania, saying it was the best part of Australia and suffered only from the fact that most of its residents had never been anywhere else and couldn't therefore appreciate how good a life they had.

So his plans had been made on the basis of consolidating his business activities there. He could do it easily, he'd said, given time and luck and skill. Ruth had blindly accepted, had never questioned even—she realised now—just how much time and luck and skill he might need.

Much less how much help *she* might be able to provide, *should* provide.

'Sometimes I wonder who is leading whom down this garden path,' he had said to her not long before the wedding. She hadn't really understood then, hadn't bothered to.

With a frightening flash of insight, Ruth realised for the first time how much work Kurtis had put into trying to make a difficult relationship workable—and how little she had really done. From the very start, he'd taken a romantic but still adult approach to their love-affair; she had started—and ended it—as a child with a child's immaturity!

The romance part of it all had overwhelmed her, or she had let it! 'But I ran when it got too tough,' she muttered to herself, and shivered at the acceptance of that thought.

Rising briskly, she found herself striding to the hallway and that mirror, the one she used only to tuck in a stray strand of hair, the one she had tried to avoid so often in the months of her separation. And in it she saw a different person ... looked into pale grey eyes and shuddered at how close she'd come to throwing away everything—everything she'd wanted and needed, everything Kurtis had worked so hard to try and give her.

'Foolish child,' she sneered, then recoiled not from the expression of the image, but from the unexpected knocking on the door only metres away.

Filled now with a sudden excitement, a world away from the terror and hostility she'd felt the night before, Ruth plunged to the door and opened it, her eyes wide, a smile plastered across her face—To find her husband standing there, hands shoved into the pockets of his jeans, a bulky sweater cloaking his muscular torso, and an expression of total uninterest on his face!

'Nice to see I've been expected,' he said, and his voice was as cool as his eyes, eyes that roved across her housecoat-clad body with the same dispassionate look he might have had for a dog in the street.

'I . . . I'm sorry. I got caught up in . . .' Ruth stopped, knowing she could never get the words out without further stammering, knowing she shouldn't bother to try.

'Uh-huh. I don't suppose there's a chance of some coffee while you get yourself together?' he said, that gravelly voice, Ruth realised, almost totally devoid of expression or emotion. Just like his eyes.

'Yes, of course. Come in.' She let him in, followed him into the small living-room, noticed how his glance took in the enormous sheaf of his letters, but noticed also how he showed no indication of pleasure that she'd been reading them—as he'd asked. Showed no indication of . . . of anything. He was a stranger, suddenly, a stranger with tired, familiar eyes, an all too familiar body, but a stranger none the less.

Ruth made coffee for both of them, trying as she did so to make conversation. It was like talking to a stone. Kurtis nodded, grunted occasionally, but gave her no help, did nothing at all to ease the growing tension.

Only after he'd drunk half his coffee in that frightening, chilling silence did he deign to string more than four words together, and that only in reply to Ruth's query—a stupid one, really—about whether she ought to get showered and changed.

'It might be an idea, unless you fancy going out like that,' he growled, and his eyes said *that* held little attraction.

'Yes...I...well, I'll go and do that,' she finally managed to say, fumbling against his coldness, uncertain of what was going on, but totally certain it was not what she wanted, not what she had hoped for.

'I could come give you a hand,' he said, 'but I won't bother. This isn't the time or the place for it.' And his demeanour made the words superfluous. Despite the fact that her housecoat gaped alarmingly, that it showed too much bosom and a great deal of leg, Kurtis's expression was like a huge neon sign flashing 'Not Interested'!

Which did nothing for Ruth's nerves as she fled to the bathroom, where standing beneath the shower didn't help either. Kurtis's coolness bewildered her, following as it did the obvious passion he'd shown the night before. It was such a dramatic change, now, to find him so totally unresponsive, especially now that she was ready to talk about his letters, ready to talk—somehow—about their relationship and its problems. Problems, she now realised, that had been greatly of her own making.

It was made worse, too, by the way the reading of his letters had somehow reawakened her sensitivity to him. As she stood with the water pouring down her hair and body, memory of showers shared kept intruding. She could almost *feel* his sensitive fingers moving along her body, soaping her, caressing her.

The touch of his fingers was like a racial memory; her breasts responded, her tummy suddenly got all hollow and she knew it wasn't the endless cups of coffee through the night, could feel that her sleeplessness contributed not at all.

The water trickling down her spine had his touch in the soft hollow at its base, droplets on her shoulders were like his touch, warm, soft, gentle. Before the brief shower was finished, her legs had suddenly gone all weak, almost unable to support her. *He* would have supported her, had done so many times. Too many, and yet not enough. Never enough.

But when she emerged from her bedroom, finally, clad in jeans and jumper, her hair still a damp jumble that would eventually dry in its usual chaos, Kurtis's uninterest continued unabated.

'I'm ready now,' Ruth said, trying to force some brightness into her voice, trying to somehow dispel the pallor of gloom that hung over the small living-room.

'For what?' he replied, not even bothering to turn from his staring out of the window and face her, oblivious to her expression, to her mood, to *her*.

'Well... to talk. Isn't that why you're here?'

'Not now.'

Blunt, direct, unarguable. Ruth stopped her next words before they passed her lips, caution and something approaching real fear thrusting tremors through her body.

'But... what, then?'

He shrugged. 'Go for a drive, a walk. Does it matter?'

'I guess not,' she replied, lying. It did matter. It mattered desperately. But what could she do? She didn't dare try to force the pace, not now. Not after all she'd done to him, to *them*.

All she could do was follow him, a moment later, out to his Porsche, mud-stained and grotty from last night's rain, and, she presumed, the long and wet trip up from Hobart the day before. He didn't bother to hold the door for her, simply slid into the driver's seat and waited silently, icily, as she fumbled her way into the once familiar car and eventually got herself strapped in.

Where are we going? she wanted to ask. But didn't. In this mood, one she'd never, ever seen with Kurtis, he might not even bother to answer. He might not know, and, worse, Ruth realised, might not care and would say so.

Or might not. Certainly he said nothing else as he drove out along Talbot Road and then turned down towards the Punchbowl, a sort of natural amphitheatre which had once held a zoo but was now simply a highly popular summer picnic spot and playground, enhanced by the small rivulet that flowed through *en route* to the North Esk River.

He stayed silent as the Porsche negotiated the narrow bitumen track down into the Punchbowl, although Ruth noticed him wincing at each of the myriad traffic humps installed to slow down those drivers who had been wont to use the twisty road as a racetrack.

And, once in the lower car park, he again seemed totally preoccupied, leaving Ruth to get out of the car on her own, and, eventually, follow along behind as he wandered towards the rivulet.

They crossed on the road bridge, then turned right and began wandering along to where a duckboard foot path led to a narrow cleft in the wall of the Punchbowl. Past the end of the duckboards, the track was so narrow, they had to walk single file, and Ruth couldn't help but recall their first walk together, when Kurtis had insisted on going behind—to appreciate, as he had put it, the view.

Not this time. He strode alone before her, seemingly oblivious to her very presence, climbing sure-footedly up the rocks to the single vantage point from where the small waterfall could be properly viewed.

Ruth followed, only too aware of his athletic stride, of how cat-like he seemed when climbing, how sure his balance. She felt almost clumsy, now feeling the effects of having been up all night, and twice slipped on the rocks, although not seriously.

Kurtis stood looking at the water for long minutes, then moved aside to let Ruth down to the edge while he climbed even higher to a narrow ledge that offered a comfortable, sunny seat once he'd cleared away a few vagrant blackberry strands.

Comfortable for him, at least. In order to join him, Ruth faced either a difficult scramble or a request for assistance, and she wasn't at all comfortable with the choice.

Throughout their walk, she had been astonishingly conscious of the fact that Kurtis had made no attempt, no gesture to take her hand, and she was surprised at how much she noticed the absence. Always when they had walked together it had tended to be hand in hand, and having him there with her but without that cast as great a pall on things as did his unusually quiet mood.

She stood looking down at the water, occasionally glancing back to where he sat, staring into space, and remembered how pleasant, how *right* it had always felt to be holding hands with him on their travels. And how wrong it now felt not to.

Eventually, however, the silence became just too much; the stillness of the narrow gorge suddenly seemed oppressive, Kurtis's immobility even more so. Ruth clambered up to a point where, if he gave her a hand, she might sit beside him.

He did so without her having to ask, which was comforting until she realised he had barely been aware, himself, of making the gesture. And once she was seated there beside him it seemed to have no effect on the shroud of silence around him.

'Are we going to talk now?'

She asked the question after the briefest deliberation. Anything, she thought, would be better than the icy quiet that was broken only by the rushing whisper of the small waterfall.

'I don't know,' he replied, his voice so quiet, she barely heard. 'I'm not sure we can talk this out, which is silly, considering I came up here with exactly that in mind.'

Ruth didn't reply; had no idea what to say, what he even wanted her to say. And when he continued, she nearly fell off the ledge with the shock of what he did say.

'You've become a stranger to me, somehow,' he said, not looking at her, not touching her. 'You've never been a stranger; even the first time I met you, when you were playing at being a kitchen witch, you weren't a stranger. It was like I'd always known you, even then. But now...'

What to say? How to say—anything? Ruth found herself holding her breath, willing her mind to help her, trying to open a mouth that suddenly seemed glued shut.

'I'm...just me,' she finally managed to blurt, only to stop as her mind freewheeled.

'Yes, but you've changed, somehow,' he replied calmly, still not looking at her. 'Something's quite different, and I can't quite figure it out. Maybe I never really knew you at all. Maybe we were both fooling ourselves, have been all along.'

A chance? A slim one, but maybe the best she'd have. Ruth didn't dare hesitate, not now!

'Maybe I've just finally started to grow up,' she ventured, her voice tentative, her eyes fixed on Kurtis, trying desperately to make him look at her somehow, see her.

And when he did, she wished he hadn't. All the response she got was one eyebrow raised in a gesture of such cynicism that he might as well have screamed 'liar' in a very loud voice.

'Maybe,' he said, in a tone that also cried out his doubts, and without another word he hopped down and turned to reach up and take Ruth by the waist, lifting her down from her perch to stand tucked between him and the high rock wall behind her.

Only he didn't, as she had expected, release her immediately. He stood, his fingers firm against her waist, looking down into her eyes with a most curious expression on his face.

And when his lips swooped to claim her mouth, instead of responding willingly, ardently, as she desperately wanted to, Ruth found herself going stiff in his arms, her mouth rigid against his assault. Because it was wrong—all wrong! His kiss was punishing, almost cruel. It was a gesture of some kind, but not of any sort she wanted or needed. There was passion involved—she was being held close enough against him to know that—but there was no tenderness, none of the rightness she had always felt with him.

She twisted in his grip, throwing her head sideways to get away from his mouth, shoving both hands against his chest to gain leverage.

'Stop it,' she cried, not sure if she was angry or afraid or just what, but certain she wanted him to stop, certain it was wrong, felt wrong, tasted wrong.

'Of course.' The words were muffled because he released her and turned away so quickly that he was actually speaking over his shoulder. Ruth found herself standing alone, her entire body shaking with the shock of it all.

Kurtis stalked away down the narrow, twisting track, only to halt and turn abruptly to face her before he'd gone ten steps.

'I apologise for that,' he said brusquely. 'I...never mind.' And he was turning again, walking swiftly and leaving Ruth to follow as he strode towards the car park.

She wanted to call out to him, to make him wait for her, somehow to make him talk to her, communicate the anger she couldn't help but see in the set of his shoulders, in the tightness of his pace. But she didn't, couldn't. In the end she just...followed.

Once in the car again, he didn't retrace their route, but drove out of the Punchbowl by the eastern exit and thence to Penquite Road and down to Station Road and the North Esk crossing, apparently driving aimlessly, without purpose and without speech.

Ruth sat silent beside him, her eyes drawn to the vista of flooded paddocks and swift-flowing water where the river had burst its usual banks and was spreading through the lowlands. As they crossed the bridge she could see that the water was nearly high enough to cause serious traffic problems if it rose much more.

Kurtis turned hard into the road which formed the entry to the picnic area on the eastern shore, an area now three-quarters under water, with picnic benches sitting like islands and the shoreline willows perched far out in the flood. He turned the small car into an elevated section of the parking area, seeking a place to get turned around, then muttered an explosive curse and halted with a jerk. Ruth, who had been staring abstractly at the flooded river, looked up to see Kurtis climbing out of the car and striding angrily round to her own side, where she suddenly realised why he'd halted.

There on the verge of the floodwaters, only inches from being swept away, was a tiny black and tan puppy, huddled and shivering despite the strong sunlight.

Ruth had her door open by the time Kurtis had picked up the animal, and could hear him speaking soothingly to the pup, who she now realised was only about six weeks old.

'You're all right, little mate,' he was saying as he cradled the pup in his arms and moved to hand it to Ruth. 'There's a bit of rag in the glove box, I think,' he said. And the fierce anger in his eyes was belied by his gentle tones as he continued then to croon to the shivering puppy.

It wasn't until Ruth had the tiny animal wrapped in the cloth and could feel its trembling begin to abate that Kurtis returned to his side of the car, got in, and let his rage begin to escape.

'Bastards...bastards...*bastards*,' he growled, shaking his head, his jaw muscles taut with his anger, his mouth white against clenched teeth. 'By the gods, Ruth, if I could ever catch the cowardly, rotten animal that would do a thing like that, I'd... Just feel that pup! He's only been there a short while. He's not wet; he hasn't been there through the night or anything.

'He was dumped there this morning, not very damned long before we arrived. And the...the *bastard* who did it didn't even have the guts to knock the poor little beggar on the head, just left him there and hoped the water would rise enough to do the dirty work for him. Oh, damn it— I hate people sometimes.'

He started the car again with a savage twist of the ignition key, and fifteen minutes later—after a stop at a phone box to check and get directions—they were pulling up outside the RSPCA headquarters in Mowbray.

Throughout the journey, and all the way back to Ruth's home, Kurtis said almost nothing, but the grinding of teeth and his obvious anger was a palpable presence in the small vehicle. It was an anger so unfocused, in some ways, that Ruth could actually feel it touching not only the unknown person who'd dumped the puppy and the system that virtually guaranteed it would end up being put down within days, but her, himself, the world in general.

'Let's write off today as a bad joke and try again tomorrow,' he said when they arrived at her home. 'You look like you haven't slept at all, and I feel about that way, so there's no sense trying to accomplish anything with us both in that condition.'

'Tomorrow's a working day,' she reminded him, venturing the words carefully, quietly, suddenly afraid of his anger, unsure how to deal with it.

'Phone in and tell them your husband's back after a long absence,' he replied with a half-grin that was too tinged with sadness to carry the joke. 'They'll understand.'

'Not likely,' she replied. 'There have to be better reasons than that to take a sickie.'

'Better a plausible lie than the reality of the truth?' he replied caustically. 'OK, phone in and tell them you've got the flu or something.'

'I don't do things like that,' Ruth replied, her own anger rising now. How dared he try to insist on such a thing?

'You can do it or I can,' he replied, and the grimness in his voice made her turn to look at him with surprise as he continued. 'I suspect a word from me would be enough to persuade Mrs O'Connor to give you the day off—the *week* off, if it comes to that.'

'A word from you?'

Ruth almost had to stifle a grin despite her growing anger. If there was one man alive tough enough to stand up to the director of the nursing home, it would be Kurtis, but over the months she'd come to know Mrs O'Connor Ruth was sure it would take far more than just a word to manage it. There would literally be blood on the floor if Kurtis and 'The Dragon' ever locked horns.

'Well, maybe more than just one, but not many,' he replied, still grim. 'I pay her salary, after all; that does give me *some* privileges.'

Ruth stared at him in stunned silence, her fears forgotten, her anger forgotten, her mind suddenly a whirling vortex of confusion. She must have heard him wrongly. She must have! If he paid O'Connor's salary, it meant that he owned the nursing home, and if he owned the nursing home it meant that he paid *her* salary as well. But that was the smallest of the implications, hardly relevant when compared to the rest.

Ruth stared and Kurtis met her stare with a calm, level gaze that held just enough smugness to make her confusion smoulder into a growing fury.

CHAPTER SIX

'YOU...you've known where I was all along.'

It wasn't a question, nor did Ruth really need an answer. She knew the answer, could feel it in the deep emptiness where her stomach had been.

Kurtis didn't bother to reply; he knew the answer too.

He merely looked at her, and now she was *certain* of that smug, cat-with-the-cream expression. And she hated him for it!

'You are a proper bastard,' she hissed, shooting him with her eyes, trying to cut his throat with her tongue. Her fingers clenched and unclenched, nails digging into her palms so hard, she half expected to find blood dripping from her hands.

Still no reply, except for the glint of satisfaction in his eyes—unless she imagined that, but Ruth didn't think so. She'd seen it before, often, when a deal had gone particularly well for Kurtis.

Frustration burned like acid inside her and she spat out her words, heedless now of his anger, heedless of anything but her own feeling of rage and betrayal and confusion.

'I suppose next you'll be saying you organised it for me to *get* the damned job,' she shouted. She wanted to reach out and tear the answer from him physically, but didn't quite dare.

The hateful raised eyebrow again, but not a word of reply. Was he deaf? Or was he simply enjoying this moment too much, taking his pleasure from her misery?

She clenched her teeth, biting back invective so scathing she dared not even use the words, while Kurtis met her eyes, now with a grin starting to play round his lips.

'You have a nerve,' he said then. 'Imagine going off and marrying a man you know so little about that you could even *think* of making an accusation like that. No, my angry little witch, you can be sure as God made little apples that you got the job purely on merit. I have my faults, but I'd never insult you by getting around your professionalism in that way—or any other way.'

'Except to organise a *sickie* for me when it happens to suit your pleasure?' she snapped. 'Or doesn't that count?'

He had the courtesy to wince, visibly, and nod his acceptance of the counter—then grinned even more widely.

'Guilty as charged, your ladyship, but in my defence may I say that I consider the salvation of a marriage more important by far than *anybody's* professionalism, including my own?'

'It's your story; you stick to it,' Ruth retorted. 'And while you're doing so, perhaps you'd like to explain things just a bit more fully. There's too much about this I don't understand and don't much like. Such as how you got involved in owning this nursing home, just for starters.'

He shrugged. 'I bought it, obviously. You would have known that, if you'd taken the slightest interest whenever I tried to explain to you how I was restructuring so that we could operate from Tasmania and I wouldn't have to be away so much.'

'Are you suggesting, then, that you *didn't* know I'd come to work here; that this is all just some weird co-incidence? Come on, Kurtis. I may be naïve, but I'm not stupid.'

'Of course I knew when you came to work here,' he growled. 'What kind of husband would I be if I didn't know? I've known where you've been and what you've been up to from the very start. Although to be fair I never did quite understand why you chose to make the switch to geriatric nursing.'

Ruth could only stare, her mind positive she was staring with her jaw hanging open, but unable to do anything about it. Of course he would have known! Nothing surer in this world, now that she knew *this* much.

'But... but why didn't you *do* something, then?' she heard herself asking. 'It's been eleven months, and you knew where I was, knew what I was doing, and you never *once* tried even to make contact—until now.'

'You told me not to, remember? You were very, very specific about that, Ruth. Besides——' and his lips curled in a ruefully, mocking grin—'I didn't think it would take anywhere near this long for you to come to your senses. I thought it was just another example of your peculiar brand of flightiness and by the time I realised the problem was much more serious than I had thought it was—well...'

'Flightiness!' The word exploded from Ruth's throat like a thunderbolt. 'You thought all this was due to *flightiness*?' She felt the bile rising, had to stop there because she was dead certain she was going to be sick, right there and then, and her pride leapt in to protect her from that.

'Why not?' And he looked so calm, so perfectly relaxed in saying it that she felt like slapping him. 'You *are* known for being a touch flighty on occasion, my lady witch,' he continued, and Ruth felt her insides tighten just at the sound of those too familiar words.

'I think that's . . . that's disgusting,' she replied.

'Quite likely. Especially since by the time I realised it was much, much more serious than just flightiness it seemed wiser just to let things continue until I had it properly figured out.'

'Until *you* had it properly figured out. Without so much as speaking to me about it, without listening to *my* side of the story, without . . .' She paused there, unable to go on, unable even to comprehend the type of reasoning behind his actions.

'Without any more to go on than that damned note!' he replied, and finally began to show irritation. 'That note, Ruth. Your note . . . the one you left for me, the one that said damn all about anything except that you couldn't take any more.'

The kind of note a child left when he or she was running away from home . . . He didn't have to say it again; the words resounded through Ruth's memory, stifling her next retort.

'Anyway, it doesn't matter now,' he was saying with what seemed to be a forced cheeriness. 'You're exhausted and I'm tired and I've had about enough of this for now. So off you go to organise tomorrow off and then get some sleep.'

'The hell I will,' she cried. 'I want to talk about this and I want to do it *now*, if you don't mind. You can't just spring stuff like this on me and then...'

'And then go off and leave you? I shouldn't, I know, because that's *your* trick. But I can and I will.' And now his grin was pure devilry. 'Unless, of course, you'd prefer me to come and *put* you to bed, which I'm equally prepared to do, although I doubt you'd be so amenable. You would, however, enjoy the experience; I can guarantee it, my lady witch.'

Ruth couldn't help herself; she reared back in alarm and yanked in panic at the door-handle, then had to meet his mocking laughter as she realised he'd quite deliberately manipulated the locking switch.

'I suppose you think that's funny,' she charged, scowling at him and trying to cover up the growing sense of panic she felt. He was more than capable of doing exactly as he'd threatened, she knew. Worse, he might just take it into his head to follow through on the threat.

And what would she do? A part of her, the part that had suddenly made her go all soft in the tummy, the part that had her lips parted and her breath suddenly short, would welcome Kurtis and his threat with open arms. But it would be nothing short of sheer folly, and she knew that in her soul, in her mind.

'Amusing, at the very least,' he chuckled. Then, to her horror, he reached over to lay his fingertips against her neck, touching at her pulse, then shifting slightly so that he could touch her just below the nape of her neck.

When she was older, he'd often said during love play, that spot would be her dowager's hump, but for now it was a convenient area that he'd found would make her knees melt at the slightest touch.

And eleven months of separation hadn't changed a thing! Ruth knew that if she were to try and get out of the car at that moment, her legs wouldn't have supported her. And to make matters worse he was giving her *that* look, the look that seemed to penetrate to the depths of her being.

'Please...don't,' she pleaded, shrugging her shoulders to free herself from the touch. 'As you said earlier, this isn't the time or the place and it isn't something I enjoy anyhow.'

Which last was a lie and she sensed that he knew it, that his sensitive fingers had already told him how quick she was to respond to his touch, to his mere presence.

'You may have changed in some ways, Ruth, but you're still a witch,' he murmured, ignoring her shrug, his fingers tracing lines of pure magic along her neck. And his eyes now held their own magic; magic that threatened Ruth because she was so totally vulnerable to it.

'No!' she cried, and reached up to fling his hand away as she would an insect. 'Stop it and stop it right now, damn you. If you won't talk to me, you sure as hell can't be wanting to do *that.*'

'Can't I? After eleven months without you, Ruth? Really...'

But he removed his hand. The light went out of his eyes and she saw him reach out to unlock the doors of the car, no longer looking at her now, no longer in tune with her thundering heart.

'Tomorrow,' he said firmly. 'And this time please try to be ready, as in *dressed* before I arrive. Let's say... eight o'clock?'

'Say what you please,' Ruth replied. 'If I'm not here, it will be because I've gone to work, which I still think I ought to do. If nothing else, I can well and truly use the overtime.'

She wasn't alone in that. A quick ring around later that afternoon found Ruth easily able to find a replacement for her Sunday shift, and someone grateful in the bargain for the overtime involved.

Ruth herself was less charitable about the whole thing, especially after Mrs O'Connor proved uncharacteristically agreeable about the change. Had Kurtis already stuck his oar in? she wondered, then compounded it by wondering if perhaps Mrs O'Connor had known Ruth's marital situation all along, but said nothing. Or been ordered to say nothing.

She made a half-hearted effort to follow Kurtis's orders and get some sleep, knowing full well he was all too right about her need for it, but the effort was time wasted. Her mind was in a whirl, her body almost worse. Just from that one touch; it shouldn't have mattered a bit and yet she couldn't get it out of her mind and shivered deliciously just at the thought.

It brought to mind also one of his rare criticisms, the words of which had stayed with her although the incident which had provoked it was long forgotten.

'If you keep this up, Ruth,' he said, 'you'll end being a repressed, middle-aged housewife.'

But *why* had he said it? Ruth found herself lying in bed, further from sleep with each passing minute, with the words revolving through her head and the reasoning behind them lost in some chaos of selective memory.

And when she wasn't thinking about that, Kurtis's involvement in the nursing home, in *her* job and without her knowledge, kept creeping in. With the benefit of hindsight, it all fitted a pattern she had noticed ever since she'd started working there, having applied for the job because a nursing friend had mentioned the place as one to look towards in the future.

'They're going places, for sure,' Ruth had been told. 'New owners, and—miracle of miracles—it seems to be somebody with crash-hot ideas about providing a proper service for the oldies without trying to become a millionaire at their expense.'

Which had certainly proved true. The home had been the subject of continuous physical upgrading all the time Ruth had worked there, with the emphasis on the patient's physical and emotional comfort rather than administrative ease. Other staff members, most of whom had worked at other such establishments and had more specific knowledge of conditions than Ruth, had continually praised both the nursing home and their jobs.

'I don't know how they can afford to do all this,' one woman had said, 'but I can tell you it's heaven compared to where I worked last. There, the poor old dears were lucky if the staff had time to help them comb their hair in the morning. Everything was price-cut to the bone and beyond and it was, quite honestly, a pig of a place to work.'

Not so Kurtis's operation. Staff morale was of the highest order and that of the patients as high as it could be, considering they were virtually all just waiting to die and knew it. That, Ruth knew, was an element that couldn't be changed, but at least their waiting could be made comfortable, dignified, and *personal*. And it was. The upgrading had been, and still was, providing vast increases in terms of personal privacy, comfort, and as many of the little touches that could, Ruth knew, make all the difference to those confined to such a facility.

During her time there, the entire catering system had been changed to provide a rotation of cooks and menus and choices, removing one of any hospital's inherent problems—the sheer boredom of the food. A diversional therapist had been appointed, and a bus with a wheelchair lift was in almost constant use, getting as many patients as possible out into the world whenever it could be managed. Staff were always encouraged—indeed instructed—to do whatever was reasonably possible to make the patients feel they were in a *home*, rather than just an institution.

Such instruction was, as Ruth knew all too well, common in almost all such institutions; the difference where she worked was that there were sufficient staff employed to allow the instructions actually to be carried out!

Mrs O'Connor, for all her dragon nickname, was a warm and compassionate person. Her strict discipline was noted for its logic and fairness, and Ruth knew there was a long waiting list for staff positions because almost nobody, once there, ever wanted to leave.

'It's the best facility of its kind in the state already,' she'd been told when she'd started working there. 'And before we're done, we'll be the best in the country—and we'll stay the best!'

It had sounded a large boast at the time, although one that she found firmly based in reality during her ime there. And if she'd known—why hadn't she?—of her husband's ownership, she would have been far less surprised.

By six o'clock, Ruth was beyond sleeping without help, so overtired and wound up that she knew it was a lost cause. So she turned off the telephone and thrust her personal principles aside long enough to gulp down a sleeping pill, even though she hated the idea.

Twelve hours later she rolled out of bed, physically refreshed but still a mental basket case. Her first thoughts were of Kurtis and his sudden change in attitude. When he'd written, when he'd first arrived, he had seemed determined to talk the problem out, to get her convinced of the error of her ways and get their marriage back on track. But then, almost the complete opposite.

'He'll probably insist on a divorce this morning,' she muttered into the bathroom mirror, yanking painfully at her hair with a brush and wishing she had the nerve just to hack it all off and be done with it. 'Damned hair,' she cursed, then allowed herself a small smile at the memory of Kurtis's descriptions—wild, rowdy, unruly, untamable. 'It's like your mind,' he'd said once. 'A little bit of taming would be an improvement, but too much would be a total and complete disaster, my lady witch. I simply can't imagine you any way but irrepressibly, irresistibly, delightfully flighty!'

Which was not, Ruth considered over her morning coffee, what he'd be likely to say today. Although she dearly wished it could be, wished she could somehow find the words to tell him how she really felt, how she *had* grown up, *had* matured, and—most importantly—*had* realised that she loved him and wanted him and wanted to make a fresh start, somehow.

Presuming, of course, she could get some straight answers about his involvement with Rosemary. There would have to be many changes, mostly in herself, if they were to put the marriage back together, but one thing Ruth did know that wouldn't change—she wouldn't, couldn't share!

And even this much presumed he'd have her back in the first place. Ruth suddenly became quite afraid that her husband's attitude had changed far too dramatically since his arrival; that something she didn't know about and couldn't quite understand had completely turned things around.

But it wouldn't matter anyway if he refused to give up Rosemary. Faced with the need for great self-examination, Ruth found she didn't totally blame him for returning to the familiarity of a woman far better suited to his lifestyle than she herself. She *had* failed him in that way, and no longer looked on the failure as being his fault.

He had asked nothing of her except to be his wife; there had been no demands for the kind of sophistication Rosemary presented, no demands for her to travel with him, to commit herself to the constant round of business functions and cocktail parties. No demands at all, really, except those she had put on herself.

Thinking back over their months together, she realised that while he had taken an active interest in what she wore—he'd said he liked shopping with her, liked to see her try things on, liked to have some input because he knew how *he* thought she looked best—he'd never once, she realised with hindsight, insisted that she buy something just because *he* liked it, had never once bought her anything himself that she had found not to her taste.

And anything he had bought had revealed his innate good taste and regard for quality. The clothes she'd left behind in her flight to Launceston were far beyond anything her nurse's salary could have paid for, the jewellery almost beyond imagination.

Ruth stared down at her hand, then reached out to twist at the plain white-gold wedding-ring which was the only significant piece of jewellery she had brought away from the marriage. She had left everything else behind, including the stunning and unique engagement ring Kurtis had commissioned, a dazzling creation of diamonds and a single, large chunk of boulder opal with its fires lifting from a matrix that was almost ebony.

'Some people say opal is unlucky, but I can't imagine anything else for you,' he'd said on the wondrous night he'd given her the ring. 'This opal is like you, with depths and fire and vivid, unique beauty, my much loved lady witch. If eyes could be truly jewels, yours would be opals.'

Some time later, he'd twitted her about some day getting her ears pierced, making a sort of joke of it, linked to his entrepreneurial skills and Ruth's habit—annoying even to her—of losing clip-on earrings almost as quickly as she put them on. Not wearing earrings at work, she was so out of the habit that she kept forgetting to keep a check on them when she did.

'When I start insisting you get your ears pierced, you'll know we're finally in the big money,' he'd gibed. 'Because I'm damned if I'll buy you the kind of earrings I'd like to buy you until I can be sure they'll stay there for a bit.'

She reached up to touch one unpierced earlobe, her eyes closed in remembrance. How often she'd tried to tell him she didn't care about expensive jewellery, expensive clothing, expensive cars, expensive anything. True, she enjoyed being able to dress more fashionably than she had, true, she loved the engagement ring and she did enjoy the Porsche, although it would never replace her own grotty little car in her affections.

But it had been Kurtis's way with gifts, rather than the gifts themselves, that had always fascinated and charmed her. He had once discovered a children's book, illustrated, of Noyes' 'The Highwayman', and had been so delighted at the find that he had invented an occasion just so that he could present it to her that very night, complete with a reading in his most flamboyant style. He had almost never returned from a business trip without some trinket, usually inexpensive but always perfect in choice, chosen for Ruth because... 'It sang to me, like you do,' he would say. Or, 'It had your name on it; I saw it.' Or, 'It reminded me of you.' His very first present to her had been a little pewter statuette of a wizard and his tame dragon—'to guard you when I'm away'—and that gift she had brought with her. It lived on her bedside table as it had from the beginning, remote, somehow, from the trauma of the marriage itself.

And you haven't done your job real well, either, little mate, she was thinking when the telephone pealed for her attention. She answered it, expecting it to be a summons from work, only to recoil from the instrument as if it had suddenly bitten her when she heard Rosemary's voice speaking to her over the long-distance bleeps.

'Is Kurtis there yet, Ruth?' said that elegant, buttersmooth voice, the very tone suggesting it was perfectly normal to be telephoning a person she disliked on a number she shouldn't know. And without waiting for a reply Rosemary continued, 'If he isn't, he'll be arriving momentarily, I expect, and when he does it's very, very important that you have him ring me.'

'You'd better give me the number,' Ruth replied, numbed by the unexpected shock, the utter surprise of having *that* woman ring her.

'Oh, he knows the number,' was the reply, in tones that said far more than the words. 'Just be sure to give him the message the instant he arrives, because it really is quite important.'

'I'll just bet he knows the number,' Ruth replied, but she was speaking to a dead telephone; Rosemary had hung up without so much as a goodbye, a thank-you or any sort of explanation.

Ruth ended up just sitting there, staring at the telephone while bitterness roiled up in her throat, a frustrating, palpable bitterness that threatened to choke her.

What a splendid job she'd made of hiding herself, she thought. Kurtis had *always* known exactly where she was, which was bad enough in itself, but to find now that Rosemary also knew—although why it should surprise her she couldn't imagine—that was adding insult to injury.

She had only just repressed an urge to throw the telephone across the room when Kurtis's familiar knock at the door brought Ruth to her feet, all thought of reconciliation knocked from her by the vividness of her anger.

'You're wanted in the herb garden,' was how she greeted her husband, and her voice, she hoped, quite clearly expressed her feelings.

Kurtis only nodded, then asked quietly, 'I suppose it must be important.'

'She said it was,' Ruth replied coldly. 'There's an extension in the bedroom if you'd rather have some privacy.'

His astonished look matched the tone of his own reply. 'From my wife?' He strode over to the telephone and was just picking up the receiver when Ruth's frustration broke through.

'It would be nice if you phoned collect,' she heard herself saying. 'I expect you'll be a while, and long-distance day rates are quite expensive.'

Which gained her an even more astonished look, but this time it faded quickly into one of a cold tenseness that matched her own. He was already dialling, but at her remark he reached his wallet from his hip pocket, pulled out a fifty-dollar note and flung it towards where Ruth was standing.

'I'd expect this might be enough for the call, and maybe some coffee, too, unless that's extra,' he growled, but didn't wait for her reaction. Rosemary must have been waiting for his call, because she answered immediately, and for the moment Ruth might as well not have existed.

Forcing herself to tune out the sound of his voice, she stomped into the kitchen, made him a cup of instant coffee from the recently boiled electric kettle, then stomped back to plunk the mug in front of him, very nearly slopping it all over the notepaper—*her* notepaper, she noticed—he had spread in front of him.

Ignoring his nod of thanks, she knelt to snatch up the fifty-dollar note, tucked it ostentatiously into her pocket with a glare at the donor, then marched from the room after gesturing first at herself and then, in a wide, expansive wave, to the outside, mouthing the word at him as she did so.

The only response was a nod, and Ruth barely saw that through eyes suddenly gone blurry with tears as she fled, so angry and hurt, she didn't care where she went, so long as it was somewhere away.

Damn him. Damn him and that woman too, she thought, slamming the front door behind her and marching down the footpath as if she actually had somewhere important to go. Damn the both of them!

She paused briefly at the roadside, eyes fixed on the sleek shape of Kurtis's Porsche, crouched like some predatory beast set to spring into action. Ruth stared at the car, her mind caught by a vagrant memory of a film, a book, *something* in which a man made a fetish of kicking Volvos. But the reasoning escaped her, the logic—had ever there been any—wouldn't come, and she turned to stride briskly away.

Her anger and energy sufficed to take her several blocks without much noticing where she was headed; then she realised she was nearing her local newsagent, and she almost smiled at the pleasure of having, finally, some vague purpose, some actual destination.

It wasn't until she'd started home, the collection of weekend papers beneath one arm, that she realised she had automatically purchased not only the local *Sunday* and the *Weekend Australian*, but others, the other papers she had known Kurtis would have bought, the papers they had so often shared as part of a Sunday morning ritual on those rare weekends he'd been home.

The realisation sent her back into her mind, into a curious mingling of fond memories with a sense of frustration at having so casually, so easily slipped back into old habits.

Ruth found herself angry with herself, yet couldn't help acknowledging the warm glow that memory of earlier, gentler times created. The memories came with their individual smells, even...especially the smell of freshly baked bread. Kurtis had, on one of his typical impulses, purchased a bread-making machine one day, delivering it to her as a present 'for us' and saying how pleasant it would be to stoke the thing at bedtime and know they could wake to freshly baked bread—'For breakfast in bed, which is bordering on pure decadence, and who better to enjoy it but us?'

Which they had—all of three times during the ten months of their here-again-gone-again marriage.

'Three whole times,' she found herself muttering, only to wonder then how many such times had been missed during the eleven months since she'd left the bread machine with the other wreckage of their time together.

Lost in her reverie, Ruth trudged back along her route and was several doors past her own before she realised it. The reason, however, became immediately apparent—the Porsche was gone!

She stood there, mouth agape, staring wildly about her in ever-diminishing circles, then downwards as if the machine might have sunk through the bitumen, and up as if it might have flown to perch in a tree. Then she mouthed several unrepeatable words about both Kurtis and his damned car and rushed inside to find the expectable, horrible, damnable note on her telephone table.

More of a letter than a note, to be fair, but, seeing that all to familiar 'Dear my lady witch' at the beginning, Ruth was too close to foaming at the mouth to be anything like charitable. She threw down the papers and snatched up the letter, meanwhile repeating the unrepeatable curses she'd only just completed. After its fury-making salutation the letter said:

Gone to Hobart. Didn't want to—*had* to!

Bad business problem. No choice, unless we want to be going hungry. Maybe best for now anyway—we seemed to be getting nowhere fast. Still, dear witch, it isn't over by any stretch of the imagination. We had too much to let it go like this.

There was a pause, a gap, a scribbling mark of the pen which Ruth couldn't decipher—if she was indeed meant to—then he continued.

I shall be back by Wednesday night. Against—I *know*—your wishes and my own better judgement I have arranged whatever time off you may want or need just in case you're tempted to come south and finish this...whatever we're doing. Doubt you will, but the offer's there. Otherwise, see you Wednesday night.

Just remember I love you, whatever you may think or have thought. If I didn't care, I wouldn't be writing this letter and I wouldn't have given you all this time to sort things out by yourself, although I now wonder if it was the right thing for me to have done. Whatever's wrong, we can fix it if we both want to, and I probably should have insisted we try together from the very start.

And he had signed it 'your—usually—obedient servant' then added a p.s. 'Sorry to have made you waste your day, but I don't know how to make it up to you...yet.'

Ruth sneered at the entire offering, at first. Then she read it again, this time trying to peer between the lines, trying to sense Kurtis's meaning, rather than just his words.

It was like trying to think while half asleep; her mind slogged through mires of despair and confusion, round and round and back and forth. Finally she gave it up for the moment and turned to idle perusal of the newspapers she'd bought.

The various articles which passed for 'news' interested her only in passing. Kurtis would, she knew, have read every word, although not with much credence. He'd been a journalist himself, once, in what he termed 'a former life,' and often bemoaned how low the profession had fallen.

'Most of this lot wouldn't have survived as copy-chasers in my day,' he'd said. 'Nobody wants to be just an honest journalist any more; they all want to be celebrities and columnists and TV superstars.'

But his knowledge of the profession had always stood him in good stead, allowing him to read between the lines, to see and comprehend what the stories *really* said, really meant.

Ruth shook her head angrily, furious with herself for allowing her mind to drift this far from the real issue, which was what she could and should do about her husband, her marriage, herself!

He was right, of course. They could fix whatever was wrong if they both tried hard enough, if they both wanted to. If they could trust each other . . . if she dared to trust him.

Did she? Ruth abandoned the papers and began to pace the room, her mind spinning. To her knowledge he

had never lied to her, never even tried. Except...
Rosemary's face leapt into focus in her mind, Rosemary's
voice sounded in her ears. There had been something
between them—there must have been, still was. They
were united in business somehow, that much she was
certain of. And otherwise...?

Ruth alternated her pacing with periodic pauses to scan
the pages, her mind seldom absorbing what she read,
turning the exercise into mindless work while she
thought, while her subconscious tried to make sense of
eleven probably wasted months. Eleven wasted months—
or was it closer to two years? she wondered then. Perhaps
the entire involvement with Kurtis had been wasted from
the very start.

But if it had, Ruth realised, she must share the blame,
must indeed accept that most of it was hers alone. Kurtis
had tried his best to be open and fair, tried to anticipate
problems before they occurred, tried to counter what he'd
instinctively felt about her *naïveté*, her feelings of being
a country bumpkin, of being unable to fit into his high-
tech, swift-paced world.

She felt, just then, a terrible, cloying sense of self-pity
and guilt, combined with an overwhelming feeling of
warmth and compassion for her husband and what she
had put him through.

Then she absently turned a page, read the caption beneath a picture that was all too familiar, and her warm
feeling turned to bitter ice.

Rosemary! Rosemary in all her stunning, sophisticated loveliness, standing with a man Ruth didn't know,
had never seen before, although his name was vaguely
familiar. But the caption said it all—he was Rosemary's
fiancé, her *recent* fiancé!

So that was why he'd made the sudden bid for reconciliation, she thought, the bitter ice turning to white-hot fury with the same acrid taste. Rosemary had finally found a man to replace Kurtis, leaving him, leaving him to return to his wife.

The room seemed to swirl around her like invisible smoke; Ruth felt for an instant as if she would faint. But she focused her eyes on the picture, on the shimmering words beneath it, on the ice inside her at the realisation of what it all meant.

Of course Kurtis wanted a reconciliation. Now that he was being removed from his ever-so-cosy relationship with Rosemary, it probably made sense to renew relations with his wife, however much of a second choice she might be.

'You fool,' she sighed to herself, only to repeat the words again and again in a bitter litany of self-loathing and contempt as she walked from the room, moving blindly towards her bedroom with the intention of flinging herself down on her bed for a good cry.

But to get there she had to pass the mirror, and her eyes trapped themselves there in passing, trapped themselves and in the process forced herself to look at herself, to look at how she was reacting, how she was thinking.

Accusing, those eyes. Staring back at her from the mirror they seemed to shout their accusations silently but no less accurately for all that.

You're jumping to conclusions again, they cried. Look at yourself; you're acting like a child. One minute you admit Kurtis was right, the next you accuse him without even the courtesy of asking for an explanation. You've never asked him for an explanation about Rosemary, except just the other day. Never! And now you use a newspaper picture to excuse yourself from taking the really hard decision, for going to him as he's asked, from sitting down like an adult and talking out your problems. He's your husband, but you treat him as if he's never been important, never... as if you never loved him at all...

Ruth wrenched herself free of the accusing, death-grey eyes, did indeed fling herself down on her bed as if to bury her head beneath the pillows, blot out all memory, deny the truth of what her reflection had told her.

But she couldn't. As she lay in a silence punctuated only by her own sobbing breaths, by the thundering of her heartbeat, she found herself coming face to face with a reality she had managed to ignore—deliberately—for so very, very long.

Kurtis had been right. From the very beginning, he'd seen her inability to face the hard decisions, her refusal to face up to herself, to her flightiness, to her tendency to jump to conclusions without proper thought, to her predilection for putting far too much into the 'too hard basket'.

He'd once asked her if she was really in love with him, or just with the idea of being in love. She'd laughed it off, as she'd laughed off so many of his serious questions, Ruth realised. So many... too many.

And now it was too late to laugh. She had only one real choice—she must go to him and try to open up her emotions, open up her thoughts, be straight with him, honest and open. She would have to allow him to see her vulnerabilities, to let *herself* see them, to accept them—or toss it all away as she had almost done already, as he had almost let her do by trying to give her the freedom he thought she could handle, the adult freedom he had mistakenly given to a child.

Ruth struggled for what seemed like hours in an insane battle with herself, with a person she knew, a person she thought she knew and a person she hardly knew at all. She was still struggling when the telephone shrilled its insistent demand to be answered, and she picked it up to hear a stranger's voice identify itself as an authority from the Launceston General hospital.

After so long, it seemed strange to hear her married name used, even stranger to answer to it while everything inside her was suddenly screaming to know *why* she was being telephoned.

'There has been a traffic accident,' the voice said, and then embarked on a raft of detail that went in one ear and out the other. All Ruth managed to comprehend was that Kurtis was there, in that hospital, as a result of the accident. And that he was alive!

She fought panic then, but only briefly, before slipping into her nurse's persona to get the clinical details, the specific details in the rigid, scientific jargon of her profession. It would have driven a layman to distraction, but for Ruth it was strangely comforting to understand exactly what was wrong, specifically what treatment was under way.

The details of the accident itself—the overloaded log truck that had spilled half its burden atop the unseen, low-slung diminutive Porsche at the edge of the southern roundabout—were beyond her, irrelevant anyway. She recalled them after she hung up the telephone and searched for her handbag, her car keys.

The important details, the real details of the Colles's fracture, fractured femur, broken nose, cuts, abrasions, she went over one by one, implication by implication, as she drove slowly, carefully, deliberately to where her husband lay injured.

She might not have learned how to be a wife, she thought, but at least she hadn't forgotten how to be a nurse. And with a broken wrist, a broken leg and various head injuries Kurtis would need that aspect of her more anyway, just now.

But when she got to the hospital, it was to find her nursing skills the least of his needs!

CHAPTER SEVEN

KURTIS'S voice was thickened, changed by the swollen, broken nose. His eyes, however, despite the effects of the pain and the pain-killers he was on, seemed little changed.

Not yet, Ruth thought without satisfaction, envisaging the black eyes he'd have in a few hours' time.

'They could put me in with your other geriatrics and I'd be right at home,' he growled, only to wince with the pain as he tried to smile with a cut and swollen lip.

'You're not a geriatric and you know it,' she found herself replying, looking at him, unsure if she should bend down to kiss him or not, hampered by her own confused emotions rather than his injuries.

Apart from the bandaged nose, his face and head revealed various other cuts and abrasions; his head had been shaved in two spots to allow wounds to be treated and his cheeks were already starting to swell, along with the cut lip. The broken left wrist was in plaster, as was his left thigh, and she could tell by the expression in his eyes that the pain-killers were starting to wear off.

'I *feel* like one,' he replied, the words muffled slightly as he tried to protect the injured lip by talking round it. 'And I'll bet I look like hell into the bargain.'

'You have looked better,' Ruth replied calmly, conscious of the voice inside her that simply wanted to scream out her pleasure that he was *alive*, that his injuries were—all things considered—rather minor. He

153

would heal, given time and patience; there was no serious, lasting damage, no disfigurement.

She took refuge in her professionalism, but no real pleasure; something in her wanted the luxury of a *normal* reaction, of tears and hugging and obvious, genuine relief. But did Kurtis want that? It was no pleasure at all to find she really didn't know.

'Does that mean you won't be applying for a job here, so that I can be assured of the very best of care?'

Was he joking? Or serious? Ruth simply couldn't tell.

'You can be assured of that without me,' she finally replied. 'And you wouldn't want me anyway; you'd be shocked to find just how unsympathetic nurses can be when their own . . . families are sick.' She stumbled over that one word, but managed none the less to keep her voice light, her attitude calm.

'So you've told me, often,' he replied in non-committal tones. 'I used to think you were probably overdoing it a bit, but . . . well, I guess I'm about to find out. Only not just now, my lady witch—now I have much more important work for you.'

More important? What, Ruth wondered, could possibly be more important? Except, perhaps, that he had changed his mind about a reconciliation, and now didn't want to be compromised in that decision by his injuries.

'Just now, the important thing is to get you fixed up, and it won't be very pleasant, I expect,' she finally managed to reply. 'You'll be a while getting out of that bed, never mind worrying about work for either one of us.'

'How long a while?' And now his eyes took on a worried look she did recognise.

'A couple of weeks, I'd say. Maybe less if you behave, which isn't something I'd expect of you,' Ruth replied. 'On the other hand, they might throw you out sooner if you misbehave too much.' She walked round to look at his chart, asking as she did so, 'Have they told you how bad that leg is?'

'It isn't crushed, apparently,' Kurtis replied with a grimace. 'The quack kept saying it was a *simple* fracture, although you'd never know it from all the fiddling around they had to do. I'll bet if it were *his* leg he wouldn't think it was so simple.'

Ruth couldn't help but smile.

'And I suppose you told him just exactly that,' she said. 'You'll be out of here sooner than you think if you go about abusing the doctors.'

'I found his attitude toward my poor broken body to be extremely... casual,' Kurtis replied. And he looked so deliberately pained by the realisation that Ruth could only shake her head and chuckle.

'You might consider he's probably seen far worse injuries today,' she replied. 'Although of course your own would be the most important from your viewpoint.'

'Too damned right they are,' was the gruff reply, followed by a vain attempt to smile round the swollen lip. 'None of which excuses a rotten bedside manner. If yours had been that bad I suspect I might not have married you.'

'Well, if I'd known you were going to be this accident-prone, you wouldn't have got the chance,' she retorted, falling in with his attitude, unable to resist his stirring, less able to ignore the light of laughter in his eyes. 'And,' she added, her own voice now choking back either tears or laughter—she wasn't sure which, 'you certainly never mentioned it in your letters, either.'

Kurtis's mouth twitched first with an attempted grin then in a grimace of pain.

'Would you?' he asked, his voice now a husky growl. 'It was bad enough having you think I was a geriatric, at the time.'

'Geriatrics,' Ruth snapped, 'are at least old enough to have some sense. They don't go about trying to argue with loaded log trucks.'

'Your crystal ball's gone all foggy again, my lady witch,' Kurtis replied, and now she noticed he was starting to fade as the drugs began to take effect. 'I didn't start the argument; I merely lost it.'

And before she could think of any reply he had reached out his good arm to grasp her wrist, pulling her close against the bedside.

'Enough of this, for now,' he said in a husky whisper. 'There is important business to discuss—*very* important, Ruth, so please let's drop the sarcasm and stirring and whatever else is between us, because I need your total attention now. OK?'

She nodded, and he continued, struggling now against the medication and his body's reaction to the shock and stress. 'I want you to go to Hobart—today,' he said, and then launched into a set of instructions that sounded like something out of a spy thriller.

As Ruth listened, first in surprise and then in genuine astonishment, his weakening voice directed her to write down what he told her because remembering was all-important.

She was to take his keys, let herself into the flat—the luxurious Sandy Bay apartment they'd exchanged for her rather too small unit in Moss Park Drive—and use the combination he gave her to get into the small safe that had been installed so secretly, she remembered, that it was reachable only through the bottom of the sink unit in the laundry.

'I'm sure you won't remember the combination yourself, although you did have it once,' he said, and had the grace to ignore her guilty blush. 'There's money in there, and a whole heap of documents, but the important thing is the little key you'll find tacked up into the top right-hand corner. You'll have to fiddle a bit to get at it, but it's there.'

Ruth nodded, her mind agog at the developing saga, question piling upon question, but none of them capable of being asked.

'Take the key, take your passport, which you somehow forgot about in your abrupt exodus,' he continued, 'take whatever money you think you might need—there should be heaps—and book yourself on the first flight to Sydney you can manage. Tonight, hopefully, but as quick as you can arrange it, Ruth, because time is vital in this.'

He grimaced and sighed with the evident sapping of his strength, but shrugged off her immediate suggestion that surely this could wait, that he needed rest more than increased agitation.

'There's a phone list on my desk. Use it—call Ro once you've got everything, or if you have any hassles, and arrange with her to meet you at the airport when you get to Sydney,' he went on, oblivious to how just the mention of that name made Ruth's hackles rise.

'But...but surely...' Ruth stammered. 'I mean...I don't know anything about your business affairs and...'

'And it's time you damned well did,' was the gruff reply, cutting off her objections for the moment. 'And don't, for goodness' sake, forget the passport; you'll need it for identification—which means you're Ruth *Goodwin*—that's important.'

Important, and slightly unnerving after nearly a year of using her maiden name, the name in which all her nursing accreditation was documented. She'd never got round to changing that, and had been glad of it when she'd fled from her marriage. Now, somehow, his comment sounded more of an accusation than he'd implied.

'But... surely Rosemary...' and she faltered only slightly over the hated name '...surely Rosemary can take care of all this. She is your partner, after all.'

Kurtis sighed, this time a sigh recognisable as being forced by frustration as much as exhaustion.

'Business partner,' he specified. 'And that only in certain very distinct areas. *You*, dear witch, are my *partner*. And this little bit of business requires both Rosemary and you, since I can't manage to front up. You, your signature, your proper identification, your status as my wife. Is that clear enough?'

Ruth hardly heard the last of it; her mind was still focused on that astonishing earlier bit about *her* being his partner. Not Rosemary—*her*!

It was a remark she knew would stay with her for a very, very long time, although whether its significance would survive their eventual decision about the future of their marriage she couldn't imagine and didn't dare try, just now.

Kurtis evidently wasn't aware of having been so profound. More visibly weakening now, he began rushing through the rest of his instructions. And now, once again, it seemed to Ruth that Rosemary was the dominant factor.

Rosemary would meet her at the plane. Rosemary would take her to a depository where keys and signatures and identifications would be needed to retrieve certain documents. Rosemary would take Ruth—who would take the documents—to where the documents could be inspected, itemised, receipted and signed for. Rosemary *should* be able to answer any queries the recipient might have.

'But you'd better take the phone number here, just in case,' he added. 'I'm not sure I can depend on my memory real well under this damned medication, but I'll manage somehow if I must.'

Then he went on to explain that for the first set of documents Ruth would be given *other* documents. Ruth would be given them, not Rosemary. And Ruth would have to sign for them.

'You needn't bother inspecting them, because they won't make any sense to you,' he said. And Ruth was sure she caught a flavour of...disappointment?...in his weakening voice.

But it wasn't important, not in comparison with her growing concern that he was over-extending himself, stretching his now fragile physical resources further than he should.

'You have to rest,' she said, only to be ignored.

'Plenty of time to rest later,' he said. 'Like you said, I'll be here a while. But there's damned little time to sort this business out—I want you on that plane today, if you can possibly manage it.'

And then, with a surprising softness in his voice, 'Only make sure you drive carefully and take care of yourself; you're more important than any business deal.'

It was, for a moment, as if he'd never said the words, as if they'd magically appeared from thin air. Ruth floated off into an instant of unreality, and when she returned he was all brusque and businesslike again, the softness gone from his voice, his eyes shadowed with fatigue but sharply focused.

The second set of documents would change hands—Rosemary would provide transportation and such introductions as were necessary—then money would become involved—real money, cash, in fairly stupendous amounts.

'Count it,' he said in a determined tone. 'You won't have to question the amount—that's already been agreed. But count it and make sort of a show of doing so, because it will be expected.'

'Count it,' she repeated, her brain starting to go into overload at the complications of the whole thing. 'And...?'

'And then Rosemary will take you to a bank, where there is a special account in my name and yours, and you will put the money into the account, get a proper receipt for it, and then the hard part's over,' he said.

'The hard part's over?' Ruth shook her head, annoyed with herself for seeming to repeat everything he said. 'OK, and then what do I do?'

'By then you'll probably be as tired as I am now,' was the reply. 'You'll most likely want to hit the sack and sleep the clock around. We don't have the flat in Sydney any more, which presents a slight problem, but Rosemary will expect to put you up if you get there tonight, so I imagine she won't mind doing it again tomorrow night if it's needed.'

Not on your life, was Ruth's immediate reaction. She would, she determined, sleep in the streets first! But she didn't say so, didn't even bother to question Kurtis's presumption. In his condition it would only cause unnecessary agitation.

She said instead, with studied casualness, 'I'm sure Rosemary will have plenty of other things to do. I see by today's paper she's just about to marry.'

Was it her comment that caused the flicker of pain so obvious to her trained eye? Or was it expectable, logical pain caused by his injuries? Ruth had to admit she couldn't tell the difference; all she could recognise was the pain itself.

But she was more than capable of deciphering Kurtis's next move, which was to reach up with his uninjured hand to draw her down closer to him, then to cup his hand round her neck, his fingers touching with deliberate tenderness, deliberate sensuousness, at the nape. The gesture caught her slightly off balance, its effect even more so, Ruth felt the tingling that seemed to flow through her entire body, tautening her nipples, flowing through her loins like liquid fire, weakening her knees so that she almost fell across his bedridden figure. She was so sensitive to his touch that she could have melted right there on the spot, but so sensitive to the emotional chasm between them, she wanted only to run, to flee.

As it was, she found herself half sprawled across her husband, hampered in her ability to get away by the need to avoid leaning on him, falling on him.

Kurtis had no such impairment, or seemed not to. His fingers played a tune of agonising sweetness at her nape, his lips moved against her cheek, sliding along her jawline to her ear.

'Remember to drive carefully,' he whispered, the very words a caress, as tangible as his physical touch. 'And remember too, my lady witch, that I love you.'

He waited then, until she had regained her balance, was upright once again and looking down at him, before adding, in quite deliberate tones, 'And remember that Rosemary isn't your enemy, Ruth—isn't and never has been.'

To which—what answer? That he was wrong, mistaken, deliberately blind, hideously biased? Ruth didn't know the answer herself, could see no logic to any reply. She could only nod, her senses overwhelmed by his physical touch and her own startling reaction at seeing him so helpless, so in pain.

'I...I'd better be getting on, then,' she said, and would have turned and left without another word. But Kurtis forestalled such action by reaching out to grip her wrist, pulling her down to where his lips, swollen and in pain, could touch her own with a softness, a sweetness her mental barriers couldn't withstand. He held her that way for hours, days, an instant, his lips as much a physical trap as the fingers that slid across her wrist in an equally deliberate caress.

'Go well, witch,' he finally sighed. 'And remember— this is important. Try and get it right.'

The final word to her fleeing back; Ruth was screaming inside herself, Run like a rabbit, but she couldn't *not* run, or she might never leave at all, she thought.

The next three hours, while she quickly packed a small bag, made the required telephone call to Mrs O'Connor, explaining the situation, outlining Kurtis's injuries, then filled up her car with petrol and began the drive to Hobart, seemed endless, timeless.

The journey south along the Midlands Highway, a journey so familiar as to be boring beyond all logic, took forever; she was harassed by every slow-poke, every labouring truck and semi-trailer, every Sunday driver puddling his way home oblivious to the traffic disruptions he caused.

And throughout she kept hearing Kurtis's voice saying 'you're more important than any business deal'.

When she got to Hobart, the simple act of unlocking the now unfamiliar door of the flat made her distinctly uncomfortable. She felt . . . not quite a stranger but even less a woman who'd spent nearly ten months living here. The aura of strangeness deepened as she rummaged through wardrobes to find clothes she'd left still hanging as she'd left them, still tidily snuggled in bedroom drawers, her jewellery all laid out in the jewel case.

'I feel like a housebreaker,' she muttered to herself, only to flinch as the sound of her voice echoed spookily through the empty flat.

And she felt more like one as she crouched in the laundry with poor light making even more difficult the task of fumbling through the combination of Kurtis's well-concealed safe.

Which, once opened, revealed exactly what he'd said it would. Her passport—the first *real* document in her married name but a document never used. At her insistence, Ruth recalled, because, much as she'd wanted a honeymoon and much as Kurtis had offered, the timing just wasn't right. Her work didn't allow sufficient time off when he could fit it into his hectic schedule. Instead of Europe or North America, their honeymoon had involved visiting Tasmania's waterfalls in a scanty series of day trips and weekends.

And the well-concealed key was there, which she tucked into her handbag with the passport. And money! Money in quantities she found quite startling in her own hands. She had seen Kurtis handle such blocks of currency before, handle it casually as so much waste paper, but when her fingers touched the manifold bundles of fifty-dollar and one hundred-dollar notes they seemed to take on a life of their own, a stunning importance she simply could not take as lightly as Kurtis did.

'I probably shouldn't keep this much cash about the place,' he'd once said. 'It would serve better out there in the marketplace earning *more* money, but sometimes... well... sometimes deals require cash; sometimes it's the only thing that will make the ultimate difference. Cash money has a power all of its own, one you can see and feel and almost taste.'

Ruth had paid little true attention then, but now, with the bundles in her fingers, she could *feel* the power in them, knew just what Kurtis had meant. And she wondered why she hadn't before, why he had never filled her hands with bundles of large bills, why he hadn't forced her to recognise their power.

She was extra careful in closing up the safe and concealing it again, suddenly all too aware of how vulnerable it might be while Kurtis was in hospital. And afterwards—where would he recover? It couldn't, she thought, be here. Not alone. But the thought of having him with her simply wouldn't come into focus when she tried to force it into reality in her mind.

Thinking about telephoning Rosemary in Sydney was no less difficult, although Ruth knew it must be done, and soon! Still, having found the number in Kurtis's office, she found herself dithering over making the call itself. Dithering, nervous, angry, but—she discovered suddenly and with not a little surprise—the anger wasn't with Rosemary; it was with herself. She had Kurtis's own words to guide her, but not enough faith in either him or herself simply to accept them.

'Accept. That's all I have to do,' she told herself aloud, making the simple statement a litany as she slowly began punching the buttons that would connect her to Sydney. Then, startling herself with the laugh it created, she glanced down to the phone and, seeing it had a memory function, Rosemary's name clearly marked, realised that would have made the process substantially simpler.

'One button—nine buttons—ten buttons. Does it really matter?' she said to herself, and continued as she'd begun. But somehow that tiny contradiction calmed her, and when Rosemary picked up her telephone on the second ring Ruth was comfortably in control.

She explained the accident, detailed Kurtis's injuries in layman's terms, then went on to explain the problem the two women now faced as a result. Rosemary was far more concerned with Kurtis's health than the business problem.

'That's easy fixed,' she said. 'Give me half an hour—less—and I'll call you back with the details. I'm on a first-name basis with practically every airline booking clerk in Sydney, so it'll be faster for me to make your arrangements from this end. You just get yourself packed and put a cab on stand-by. I'll get back to you soonest.'

Then she left Ruth holding a silent telephone and silently cursing herself for forgetting to make her *own* airline booking before telephoning Sydney.

'Flighty,' she muttered, then changed the word to just plain 'stupid' and repeated that over and over as she stared out of the window at the Derwent estuary with its scattered confetti of varying sails, her mind numbed by the rapidity of events.

She thought of phoning the hospital, only to drop the idea because it might tie up the telephone just when Rosemary might try to reach her. There wasn't really anything to pack, either, she thought, then realised she might need clothing substantially more sophisticated than what she had brought with her.

Surely she would! The real impact of Kurtis's instructions suddenly struck her, and she spent ten minutes going through drawers and wardrobes to put together two business outfits from clothing she'd left behind in her fleeing.

A two-piece suit in ivory and black, the fabric sleek and clinging, but ideal for travelling in being uncrushable, never needing ironing. She had missed that outfit, she now admitted to herself, more than any other in the left-behind wardrobe. And the other was a warmer, slightly more sedate blazer and skirt in basic navy with vivid scarlet underpinnings and a blouse which carried through the colour scheme.

It felt strange, somehow, sorting through clothes that had become relics of a shattered relationship, a part of the past now yanked into the present through necessity. But it felt even stranger, Ruth found, when she pulled open what had been her lingerie drawer to find vivid, more intimate memories flooding out in a riot of colour.

A memory more than two years old but fresh as morning reached out to touch her, and the reaction was much the same as when Kurtis had touched her neck with his fingers.

The first time he had brought her a present of lingerie, sleek and frilly and almost indecently scanty and ten times more expensive than anything she had ever remotely considered for herself, she had been torn between embarrassment and naïve shyness, almost balking at his laughing insistence on an immediate modelling.

'It won't take long, because I intend to take it right back off you and then make mad, passionate love to you,' he'd said, and the gleam in his eyes had matched his grin, the tenderness of his touch at her throat.

There had been a special intimacy, then, in the touch of the cool silk against her skin, a touch somehow as delicate and sensitising as that of Kurtis's fingers. Her shyness had risen to the bait of the minuscule suspender belt, the unfamiliar difference in the feel of stockings instead of tights. But it had been compensated for, and more, by the look of admiration as Kurtis had watched her, caressing her with his eyes, and she had finally thrown back her shoulders and strutted, revelling in the effect despite knowing he had created it as much as she.

'I don't ever need reminding that you're very much woman indeed, my lady witch,' he'd said in a whisper against her ear as he slowly, delicately, began to reverse the process she'd only just completed. 'But you, on occasion, on the blue and bad days, might just find it nice to be reassured.' Then he'd laughed, a booming, lusty, comfortable laugh, and added, 'Besides, it's the kind of gift that can always guarantee to be for both of us.'

And it had begun a love-game between them, a tradition that had evolved from the first time she'd collected him at the airport wearing what he called her 'pedestrian underwear', the very utilitarian, basic underwear she had always worn with her uniforms.

In the very process of hugging her, kissing her, his fingers had crept tantalisingly down her back, then halted abruptly as they somehow detected the difference between sultry silk and sensible cotton. His whispered suggestion concerning the bra's immediate future had left Ruth gasping with surprise and laughter, but the seriousness of his attitude was never in question.

'You can wear that sensible, pedestrian stuff for work if you must,' he'd said on the way home. 'But never, *never* when you're going to be with me, unless you want to cause a serious and immediate domestic when I remove it from your wondrous body and cut it into very, very tiny shreds. Do I make myself clear, my mistress lady witch?'

Ruth allowed herself a chuckle at remembering her flamboyant response.

'I don't see much difference—you take the fancy stuff off just about as quick,' she'd quipped, only to have him reach across to put a hand on her thigh and murmur in overdone, sultry tones,

'Ah, no...slower. Much, much slower. When we get home, my love, I shall demonstrate.'

And he had. Ruth found herself remembering that wondrous occasion, her fingers idly stroking the fabric of a crimson silk chemise, when the ringing telephone brought her back to reality.

'It's all organised—the plane leaves in an hour and a half; your ticket will be waiting for you. You've got money to pay for it? Right, see you when you arrive; just go straight out the front door and watch for a white BMW... See you.'

Rosemary's expectably efficient arrangements were delivered with gunfire rapidity, with no opportunity for Ruth to broach the subject of where she would stay that night or the next. And now, Ruth accepted, was hardly the time to worry about it.

She telephoned for a taxi to be there in twenty minutes, finished her packing in five, then took five more to check on Kurtis, who was resting and best not disturbed, she was told.

Still with time to kill, she found herself prowling the flat, some impression tugging at her subconscious as she opened kitchen cupboards, inspected the contents, feeling more and more like a prowler, a stranger.

It was some minutes before she realised that she was seeking information that simply didn't exist—evidence of a woman's presence in the flat that had been her home. And there was none. The refrigerator contained only the expected minimum she knew Kurtis would have maintained. She drank the half-litre of milk, discarded one or two items of questionable freshness, then shut it again. The freezer held no more than half a brick of butter and several packages of the pork spare-ribs he loved to cook for himself as a special treat.

Ruth could tell from what she saw that he'd been away a good deal and eating out most of the time otherwise, as well. The fact that the entire flat was clean and tidy was only what she would have expected from her husband; he'd often joked that he was twice the housekeeper she was, and had got no arguments on the subject.

The taxi arrived just as she was debating what of *his* clothes she ought to pack to take back to Launceston with her, having only just realised she had no memory of seeing his suitcase in the hospital room, or of having enquired about that aspect of things as she ought to have done.

'Flighty,' she muttered as she scampered down to meet the taxi and begin a Sydney journey that promised to be even stranger than her first.

Just how much stranger she didn't appreciate until her arrival, when she walked out of the terminal to find Rosemary's car miraculously double-parked and waiting. And the driver herself, turned out perfectly as always in the latest of business fashion, waved gaily at Ruth's approach, seemingly oblivious to the hostile glares of taxis queuing at the terminal and motorists searching for people with far less than Rosemary's success.

'I wasn't sure if you'd have the chance, so I checked the hospital and he's doing fine,' were Rosemary's first words. 'The only problem is that his suitcase disappeared in the confusion so he's only got the clothes he was wearing, which is no problem just now, but he'd like you to pack him some gear when you get back.'

Ruth shuddered inwardly at the remark, her own guilt leaping to the bait, however unintentional. Then she bit back her bile and managed a polite thank-you. But nothing, she thought wryly, could have been more calculated to put the final touches to an already horrendous day.

She was wrong, and found *that* out before they'd cleared the airport traffic area.

'Businesswise, it's a good thing you weren't with Kurtis. And personally too, of course,' Rosemary hastily added. 'But really, what a bummer! First I wreck your holiday by *having* to call about business, and then the accident...'

'Holiday? But I wasn't on holiday; I live there. I've lived there for eleven months,' Ruth replied absently, only to gasp in surprise as Rosemary, obviously totally distracted by the comment, nearly sent them into the ditch.

'Oh, dear. I see I've put my size nines in it right up to the ankle this time,' the elegant driver said after a most inelegant curse at her inattention.

But it was her next startling remark that had Ruth's head spinning in astonishment.

'Damn Kurtis anyway,' Rosemary snarled. 'He might have told me... but then of course he wouldn't. Not your boy.'

CHAPTER EIGHT

'YOUR boy... your boy... your boy...'

The words pounded in Ruth's ears with the regularity of a drumbeat that matched the sudden thumping of her heart. This, she thought, was surely insanity, surely...

She looked across to where Rosemary, having dropped a bombshell and followed it with another, equally implausible statement, now was concentrating on her driving.

'Do you mean to say...?' Ruth could hardly find the words, the concept of what she was thinking was so... astonishing. She fell silent, then stammered out another attempt with equally little success.

'I presume you're trying to ask if I didn't know you and Kurtis had... what? Split up? No, Ruth, I didn't know. How could I?'

'I... I just would have expected you... you would, that's all,' Ruth replied, still in a mild state of shock at having all her assumptions turned upside-down.

Rosemary took her eyes from the traffic only briefly to look at Ruth, but it was a look that combined frustration and, quite surprisingly, genuine pity as the elegant older woman shook her head.

'You, my girl, are in big, big trouble, I think,' Rosemary said with a tinge of sadness in her voice. 'Very big trouble, if you know your husband so little that you'd think he'd discuss anything so... so *personal* as that with... with me or anybody else.

'Of course now that you mention it, I can look back at the number of times I had to leave messages on the answering machine at times when you really *should*, logically, have been there. But of course I was so used to using the answering machine to reach Kurtis that I never noticed.' Again she took her eyes off the road long enough to peer at Ruth, then added, 'And I suspect that, whatever's wrong between you, you're as in love with him now as you've ever been.'

Ruth's reply was snorted down.

'Don't even bother to answer. We'll be home soon, and I think I'll pour a drink into you and let you give me chapter and verse in circumstances where I can pay attention,' she said. 'You get started now and all we'll accomplish is to have us in the ditch, so don't even start.'

'But... but...'

'I said don't start,' Rosemary insisted. 'I'll drive much better without you blatting at me.'

Then, suddenly, she smiled, and it was a smile Ruth found strangely comforting, surprisingly gentle and wise.

'If it's any consolation,' Rosemary said then, 'I *can* tell you that whatever your reasons—and I'll bet you almost any money I can list most of them without another word from you, my girl—you'll realise by the time this night's over that you've been very, very, very stupid!'

'I already know that, I think,' Ruth admitted.

'Good. It's a start, if nothing else,' was the gruff reply. 'Now shut up and let me drive.'

A command Ruth was glad to obey. Her head was swimming with confusion, her mind barely able to function at all. Rosemary's few comments had thrown her for a loop to the point where she simply didn't trust herself to make sense of anything.

It wasn't until they'd reached Rosemary's flat, which Ruth knew to be in the same large complex where Kurtis had lived when she first met him, and her hostess had quite literally pushed her into an armchair and put a large glass of Riesling in her hand, that Ruth's numb brain actually began to look like functioning.

'Kurtis *said* you weren't the enemy.'

It was all she could think of, somehow, to say. And how she expected Rosemary to understand Ruth couldn't imagine herself.

'Well, I'm glad of that much,' was the reply, accompanied by a wry grin. 'Not, of course, that you believed him. No, of course not, and that's my damned fault, along with the added sin of never even noticing. My apologies, Ruth. I have been a bad, bad girl.'

'You? It's I who should be apologising.' Ruth intended to add that her apology was due both to her husband and to Rosemary, but she was forestalled.

'To Kurtis? Yes, and you'd best make it a good one,' Rosemary replied. 'How long did you say?'

'Eleven months.' Ruth had to whisper her reply; she was hurting so much inside, now, that the sound of her own voice declaring the length of her stupidity was too much to bear.

'Hmmph!' Rosemary sniffed, rose to her feet and stalked around in a brisk, angry circle, reminding Ruth of a leopard debating whether or not to eat its prey.

'Well, before you get into "true confession" mode,' she said then, 'I think I'll blow your tiny mind by telling *you* where it all came apart and why. It'll save you having to weep and wail and gnash your teeth too much, and probably save a bit of time, too.'

Ruth was in no condition to argue. Even with the easing powers of the wine, her stomach was doing flip-flops and she found herself casting a cautious eye round to check where the loo might be found in case she needed it in a hurry.

'Let's go back to the beginning,' Rosemary said. 'My beginning, anyway, which was that wondrous weekend you spent with Kurtis and his wonderful gee-whiz electronic gadgetry. And—at least partly—with me!

'Lord, but I'm a bitch,' she growled, shaking her pristine cap of hair into a tangle that still, somehow, managed to maintain an aura of elegance. 'A proper, mean, conniving, scheming, rotten bitch! And I am sorry about that, Ruth. I know it's far too late to apologise, but it's about all I *can* do at this point.

'There you were, barely into figuring out the start of your relationship with what had to be one of the most complex men in the civilised universe, and there I was, doing my level best to bitch it up. And why? Well, not, you probably *now* won't be surprised to learn, because I had any claim on him myself. Oh, we had a sort of a start of something once, but it was a very small thing and a very long time ago, I can assure you. And not a relevant thing, either.'

Again, that curious little stalking exercise, then Rosemary flung herself into a chair facing Ruth. 'Hindsight's a wonderful thing,' she said soberly, then added, 'And if I start to sound like Kurtis at times, by the way, don't be offended or surprised. He taught me all I know and it would be amazing if I didn't.

'That,' she said with an expansive wave of one per-fectly-manicured finger, 'is why I was so damned bitchy and intrusive that weekend. Not sexual jealousy... well... maybe a bit. You'd have to grant me a bit with a man like Kurtis involved. But really, Ruth, it was far more commercial jealousy, business jealousy—call it terror, if you like.'

'Terror? That's a bit... strong, isn't it?'

'Not when you look at it from my viewpoint, it isn't,' was the deliberate reply. 'You, of course, probably haven't the faintest idea what I'm on about. Even now.'

And she shook her head, her laugh sour with bitterness.

'I'm going to have to apologise to him too,' she said. 'And it will be just as hard for me, although probably not so important. But just from your reaction I can see that I'm responsible for a lot of this whether I truly intended it or not. Eleven months! You'd best have a better explanation than I expect, girl, or else be prepared to admit you've got mush for brains.'

'I'd admit that now,' Ruth said.

'I'd rather have you admit you still love him, before this gets much further,' was the curious reply, and Ruth found herself rearing up almost angrily to reply.

'But of course I do. I... I...'

'Enough. A simple answer is always best when you're in it up to your neck,' Rosemary said. 'A quote you've no doubt heard, in perhaps more colourful language, somewhere before. You really aren't too bright some-times, are you, Ruth? I find myself looking at you now and wondering how the hell you could have terrified me so thoroughly.'

Whereupon Rosemary rose languorously to her feet, plucked Ruth's empty glass from nerveless fingers, and strode off to create a refill. Ruth sat silent, her hand unmoving, until Rosemary returned and put the glass in it again.

'You did have me terrified,' she then said bluntly. 'Kurtis came back from that first Hobart trip...changed, somehow. But he's so damned secretive about personal things I never got any details, just vague generalities about this "witch" he'd met and somehow become enamoured of. And the letters! Well! Of course I never read one, nor did I want to, seeing the effect they had on him. He was like a schoolboy in the midst of puppy-love, for goodness' sake. He kept smiling a lot, and laughing, and being all...well...not himself.'

Rosemary shook her head as if the very memory was too much to bear. 'Not himself...yes. That's one way of putting it, anyway. I got to the point where I could tell by the look of him whether you'd deigned to write or not. And to avoid being my usual smart-alec self on the days you hadn't, let me tell you.'

Ruth couldn't help it; the description so fitted her own response to the letters that she had to smile. Rosemary was not amused.

'Smile if you want to, but it was hell for me,' she continued. 'Not that it seemed to affect his business judgement, nor even his common sense in general, to be fair. Except where women were concerned. After your first visit, I don't think he ever so much as *saw* another woman, which ought to be wonderful for your ego. And he wasn't looking around much just *before* your visit, either.'

Rosemary scowled angrily, then rose to prowl the room before finding and lighting a cigarette, only to scowl even worse having done so.

'Filthy habit,' she snapped, stubbing the thing out in a fit of obvious pique. 'So is being in love—if you happen to be on the outside looking in. Which I was, at the time, and let me tell you I hated every minute of it. Not because I was in love with Kurtis, although that would have been easy enough, but because I wasn't in love with anybody!

'And there you two were, lost in a magic world of your own making, with my boss and business partner writing *love letters*, for goodness' sake.

'Well, I'm sorry, Ruth. It shames me to admit it but I was so damned cranky I just couldn't help being bitchy. I'm inclined that way anyway—you almost have to be to survive in that jungle out there.'

And she waved expansively towards the window and the lighted canyons and sparkling harbour outside. Something inside Ruth reached out to her then, feeling the loneliness, the aloneness Rosemary must have felt.

'But it wasn't only you,' she protested. 'It was...well...it was everybody. Everybody from...well, from *his* world, your world, the high-society, sophisticated world you have here. They all treated me like some sort of social pariah, and Kurtis never even seemed to notice.'

'Of course not. He's a man, after all. He was so besotted with you—*is* so besotted with you—he simply assumed everybody else was too. And if he did notice, it would only have been to see how green-eyed jealous everybody was of you.'

'Jealous? Of me? You've got to be joking,' Ruth scoffed. 'They laughed at me is all, the little country mouse going about in town, staring up at the tall buildings, overwhelmed by it all.'

'And so totally comfortable in your own skin that you made everybody—including me, which takes a fair bit of doing—absolutely green with envy,' Rosemary said. 'And that's besides the face of you having totally bewitched one of the city's most eligible bachelors. Lord, Ruth, you had all the so-called ladies in this so-called social swirl so envious I'm surprised they talked to you at all.'

'Most of them didn't,' Ruth said.

'And you, very wisely I must say, only turned up here on rare occasions anyway, thus keeping yourself sufficiently a mystery that nobody ever got the chance to figure you out.'

'I, very *unwisely*, let my own fears and insecurity keep me from being with my husband, where I should have been, thus creating all sorts of problems.'

Rosemary shook her head sadly.

'Like jealousy on your part, which isn't hard to understand, considering how much he was away. Well, you can forget about that bit, Ruth. Kurtis simply isn't the type. I'm surprised, though, I must admit, that you let yourself be led down that little garden path.'

'I was sure . . . sure it was you,' Ruth finally managed to say, stumbling over the words, over the sheer idiocy of the thought, now that she and Rosemary were sitting here, face to face, and actually *talking* to one another. Which, she realised, is what should have happened in the first place. Even before she and Kurtis had married, there would have been opportunities. She could have *made* such opportunities, had she had the sense. 'And that wasn't your fault; it was mine,' she hurriedly added, staving off whatever Rosemary was about to say. 'I jumped to a conclusion, then bound myself into the situation without even considering I might be wrong.'

Now it was her turn to shake her head wearily, sadly.

'Flighty. That's what Kurtis would say. I'm beginning to think just plain stupid is a better description.'

'Ah, yes. Kurtis. We'd best not forget about him. Not that you're likely to. I presume from the way this is shaping up that you never bothered to enquire of *him* where his preferences lay.'

The sarcasm wasn't totally wasted. Ruth felt the colour rising in her cheeks, but refrained from snapping too obviously at the bait.

'I…well, what would you expect?' she replied. 'What was I to do—tie him to a chair and shine bright lights in his eyes and demand to know the exact nature of his relationship with you?'

A waste of angst. Rosemary's laughter tinkled through the room before she said, 'Probably easier just to ask him, although I'd be surprised if you were forced even to do that. My logic says Kurtis would have told you without being asked; he'd have made damned sure of it, my girl. Want to tell me why you didn't listen?'

Ruth was mortified, suddenly also very, very ashamed.

It was a situation that didn't improve, couldn't improve, but in the face of Rosemary's warmth and consideration she found herself talking, going on and on as if her mouth were under somebody else's control, until she had even revealed the incident of the parcel with the mousetrap and the sprig of rosemary.

That proved too much even for her hostess's elegant poise—Rosemary howled with laughter, to the point where she only just managed to set down her wine glass before she was rolling about on the carpet, her eyes filled with tears and the room resounding to her cries of delight.

She had chuckled at the fact of Kurtis buying the nursing home without Ruth even knowing when she got her job, but the mousetrap story she declared the definitive winner.

'Oh, I love...I love it...I love it,' she chortled. 'And this, I can tell you, Ruth, is my punishment for being such a bitch. Just imagine having such a wonderful story—about Kurtis, of all people—and not being able to tell it? Oh, it's too much. My system will never stand it.'

'It is not,' Ruth insisted, 'anywhere near that funny.'

'I think it's the funniest, most romantic, most wonderful thing I've ever heard,' was the reply. 'And what's more I'll bet you any money he eventually described it as a "definitive statement", didn't he? Well, didn't he?'

Ruth didn't have to answer. Indeed, she would have had trouble doing so, because now the humour of the thing had got to her, too, and she joined Rosemary in laughter.

But when the laughter was over, so, surprisingly, was the depth of intimacy they had shared.

'Kurtis and I have been friends and business associates for a long, long time,' Rosemary said. 'Which explains why I'm so much more...why I may seem to know him better than you do. Do you know what I mean?

'And that's why,' she said at Ruth's nod, 'I'm going to stop this entire subject right here, right now. I wouldn't have started it if it weren't for the fact that I'm as far from my normal bitchiness as I'll ever get, right now, being madly, wonderfully in love myself, and therefore prone to the same idiocy as you've been going through. And some of what you're going through—*have* gone through—I expect I've yet to learn. I told you earlier that I didn't even know you'd split up—because Kurtis would think that something too personal, too…intimate to be discussed even with me.

'It's one of the things I respect him for, and I expect you do, too, so this conversation we've had must remain totally between the two of us. The two of us,' she repeated, then added, 'And him, of course. You must tell *him* about it; it wouldn't be right not to, and he'd be furious if he ever found out it happened and you hadn't told him. Honesty and openness and communication are everything, Ruth—absolutely everything! I'm learning that in a big way myself now, with *my* man, who's very like Kurtis in that way.'

'I have a lot to tell him,' Ruth admitted. 'But first we have to get this business over with tomorrow or I'll be too ashamed even to go back to Tasmania. And honestly, Rosemary, I haven't the foggiest idea what it's about or how to conduct myself or… anything!'

'Not to worry. Just follow my lead and I'll coach you through it so smoothly, nobody will ever even suspect. Did you bring some fairly posh clothes—real power-dressing stuff?'

She totally approved of the choices Ruth had made before leaving Hobart, then poured them each a final glass of wine and spent half an hour going over the agenda for the next day.

'Apart from that, you know as much as I do,' she finally concluded. 'This one was mostly Kurtis's doing. And the last, I might point out, that we were involved in together.'

'It seems all so...cloak-and-dagger,' Ruth said. 'I admit I haven't taken as much interest in the business end of things as I should have, but isn't this just a bit over the top?'

'It is,' Rosemary admitted. 'But only because of some of the people involved. Big money makes for big paranoias, but, on the other hand, just because you're paranoid doesn't mean they aren't out to get you.'

'If we're going to stay friends,' Ruth retorted, 'you're really going to have to stop quoting my husband.'

CHAPTER NINE

'YOU said *that* to Ro—and didn't get back-handed across the room? You don't know your luck, Ruth the witch. I'd have worse injuries than the log truck gave me if I'd dared say such a thing.'

Kurtis, looking for all the world like a racoon with his two black eyes and still swollen nose, winced at the pain caused by his astonished response.

'Rosemary is very much in love; I expect it's made her less dangerous,' Ruth replied calmly. 'It's said to have that effect on some people.'

She was sitting hard up against the hospital bed, the fingers of her left hand numb because Kurtis had been holding it tightly in his one good hand ever since she'd walked into the room. Beneath his fingers, the unaccustomed tightness of her engagement ring, which she'd worn throughout her Sydney visit and still didn't even know if he'd noticed despite his grasp, was biting into her finger with a pleasant pain.

Because of the black eyes, it was almost impossible to read Kurtis's expression. He peered out at her as if from two identical smoke-blackened caves.

Ruth had been in the room only a few minutes, and except for a brief, perfunctory and quite *correct* kiss on his cheek upon arriving, the only physical contact between them was the hand-holding. Ruth was holding herself in reserve, deliberately, until she had fulfilled what she considered her 'business' commitment. Except for the hand-holding, of course. That she treasured, totally comfortable now with everything holding hands with Kurtis meant to her, had from the very beginning.

If Kurtis was surprised by this curious combination of intimacy and business brusqueness, he said nothing. But his grip never slackened, nor did the warm glow that seemed to emanate from him as Ruth related a blow-by-blow account of her expedition.

'It was you that had such a strange, calming effect on me—not just being in love,' he said, his voice husky, but Ruth shushed him before he could continue.

'Don't interrupt; this is important. You told me so yourself before I left.'

'But you've done the business,' he said. 'It isn't necessary to go over it item by item. You have to have done exactly what was required or you'd still be there.'

'Rosemary and I had a very long talk before we got down to *business* business,' Ruth said as if he'd never spoken. 'The result of which was, to make a long story short because you're getting tired and ought to rest, that I have a long and very sincere apology to make to you. And a complaint!'

'Well, you'd better give me the apology, at least. The complaint might have to wait; you surely don't intend to pick on me when I'm bedridden!'

'I'm a nurse. I have ways that won't leave a mark and nobody will ever know,' she replied. 'Now stop interrupting, because this is serious.

'You were right about my running away. It was very immature and very unfair to you and I really have no excuse except that it was...it was...'

'It was too soon,' he prompted in a very small voice, then cringed away from her in a tragic-comic effort, Ruth knew, to diffuse her nervousness, to spare her feelings.

'Yes,' she replied soberly, ignoring his antics. 'It was too soon and you know it. You tried to make me see it, too, or at least to consider it—your letters...*damn* those letters anyway; they're going to haunt me forever.'

'As they were intended to, my lady witch.'

And *now* she could read his eyes, not that she needed to. The pressure of his fingers was enough.

'I realise that now. As I realise that I should have taken them more seriously from the beginning. And as I realise I should have given *you* more serious replies,' she said.

'I kept hoping you would.'

'Yes, you did. That was obvious. There you were, pouring out all your feelings, telling me *everything* about the way you felt, the way you thought about things, your beliefs, everything! And all I could do was give you frivolous, superficial little notes in reply.'

'Because you found it difficult to express your feelings.' He shrugged, grimacing at the effort but never loosening his grip on her hand.

'Because I didn't *want* to,' Ruth insisted. 'Oh, I haven't got your fluency with words, but that wasn't the point. I just...didn't...want to! I wanted love to be...love. I didn't want the serious part, I didn't want to worry about the future, or even consider it. Not the way you did. I was a child and I treated it childishly!'

Now, as she paused, Kurtis merely looked at her. His lip had become even more swollen since she'd seen him first, and his attempts at any sort of smile were clearly painful. But his fingers spoke for him, as did his eyes, and both shouted understanding as Ruth painfully related the problems of their marriage, the fact that she *hadn't* been able to accept his long and frequent absences as she had promised, as she should have. The problems with his work-social colleagues, the slights, the rudenesses, the innuendoes. And the main problem—herself, her immaturity, her refusal to face up to herself.

There was a slight gasp of... surprise? when she had to force herself to meet his eyes and admit that their sex life had been so wonderful, so totally exquisite, so magical that she had difficulty accepting it, believing it could last, believing it was even real.

'I think towards the end I was even a little afraid of it,' she heard herself admitting. 'And not just because I was sure I was... sharing you. It was just... too good to be true.'

His gasp was followed by a slow, knowing nod, then a minute shake of his head.

'Knew something was going wrong, but I couldn't figure it out,' he said, speaking into an embarrassed silence. 'Tried to be more gentle, more patient...'

'Patient!' Here, finally, was a God-given excuse for Ruth to launch into the second part of her performance—the complaint! 'Patient is not the word for it,' she exploded, not angrily but in an almost joyous sense of relief at having the opportunity now and the guts to get this poison out of her.

'That damned patience of yours, Kurtis, was part of the problem too,' she said. 'You were *too damned patient*! Oh, my love, why couldn't you have used a little less patience and borrowed some of my immaturity? Maybe then you could have jolted me into reality, somehow.'

'Not my style,' he said with a rueful shake of his head. 'All I can be is what I am—that's one of the reasons I was so verbose in my letters, trying to explain *everything* to you, all my flaws and faults and worries and...'

'And a lot of other wonderful things I didn't understand at the time, because they were so... serious. And I wasn't and didn't want to be. I just wanted to love you and be loved by you,' Ruth said.

'And now?'

Ah, she thought. Now it's crunch time. And she consciously squared her shoulders and leant closer, meeting his eyes fearlessly, if not quite confidently.

'Now I just want to love you and be loved by you. And now I'm old enough,' she said. And she watched his eyes, hardly daring to hope that she would see that sea of tenderness rising in them.

Nor did she! What she saw was even more important—the tide of laughter—warm, gentle, intimate laughter that was so much a part of Kurtis in her own eyes.

'Your damned timing hasn't improved much since the start of this magical romance, my lady witch,' he growled past his swollen lip. 'You finally get your cauldron working properly and look at me! I'm such a mess I can't even do anything about it. I can't even kiss you properly without getting a local anaesthetic first. Some witch you are!'

Ruth smiled, the relief probably obvious on her face and in her eyes and voice, but all the more welcome for that.

'Wait until I get you home,' she said, 'and you'll see what kind of magic I can make. Nursing and witchery make a very, very strong combination; you'll see.'

To which Kurtis raised his plastered wrist and used it to point to his plastered thigh.

'Like this? You'll need more than magic.' But now his eyes smiled and the fingers that held her own were moving, tracing runes along the sensitive inner skin of her wrist. Ruth merely smiled and reached down with her free hand to draw intricate designs along the plaster on his thigh, leaning forward until their noses almost touched as the designs left the upper edge of the cast.

'So little faith,' she whispered. 'It's no wonder you're only an apprentice-grade warlock.'

'Does your magic include being able to lock doors?' he sighed raggedly a moment later. 'What if the nurse should walk in, after all?'

'The nurse *is* in,' she replied. 'And she locked the door on her way. Surely you're not about to question my knowledge of hospital procedures, too?'

'I was about to question nothing at all, my lady witch and wife,' he said some moments later, his voice now extremely ragged. 'Besides, it wasn't ever your magic that was at issue. Only your sense of timing.'

Ruth lifted her head to stare at him, her lips curled in a broad smile.

'You want to complain about *that*?' she demanded. '*Now*?'

And joined him in howls of laughter when the answer came not from Kurtis, but as a knock on the door.

OFFICIAL RULES

PRIZE SURPRISE SWEEPSTAKES 3448

NO PURCHASE OR OBLIGATION NECESSARY

Three Harlequin Reader Service 1995 shipments will contain respectively, coupons for entry into three different prize drawings, one for a Panasonic 31" wide-screen TV, another for a 5-piece Wedgwood china service for eight and the third for a Sharp ViewCam camcorder. To enter any drawing using an Entry Coupon, simply complete and mail according to directions.

There is no obligation to continue using the Reader Service to enter and be eligible for any prize drawing. You may also enter any drawing by hand printing the words "Prize Surprise," your name and address on a 3"x5" card and the name of the prize you wish that entry to be considered for (i.e., Panasonic wide-screen TV, Wedgwood china or Sharp ViewCam). Send your 3"x5" entries via first-class mail (limit: one per envelope) to: Prize Surprise Sweepstakes 3448, c/o the prize you wish that entry to be considered for, P.O. Box 1315, Buffalo, NY 14269-1315, USA or P.O. Box 610, Fort Erie, Ontario L2A 5X3, Canada.

To be eligible for the Panasonic wide-screen TV, entries must be received by 6/30/95; for the Wedgwood china, 8/30/95; and for the Sharp ViewCam, 10/30/95.

Winners will be determined in random drawings conducted under the supervision of D.L. Blair, Inc., an independent judging organization whose decisions are final, from among all eligible entries received for that drawing. Approximate prize values are as follows: Panasonic wide-screen TV ($1,800); Wedgwood china ($840) and Sharp ViewCam ($2,000). Sweepstakes open to residents of the U.S. (except Puerto Rico) and Canada, 18 years of age or older. Employees and immediate family members of Harlequin Enterprises, Ltd., D.L. Blair, Inc., their affiliates, subsidiaries and all other agencies, entities and persons connected with the use, marketing or conduct of this sweepstakes are not eligible. Odds of winning a prize are dependent upon the number of eligible entries received for that drawing. Prize drawing and winner notification for each drawing will occur no later than 15 days after deadline for entry eligibility for that drawing. Limit: one prize to an individual, family or organization. All applicable laws and regulations apply. Sweepstakes offer void wherever prohibited by law. Any litigation within the province of Quebec respecting the conduct and awarding of the prizes in this sweepstakes must be submitted to the Regies des loteries et Courses du Quebec. In order to win a prize, residents of Canada will be required to correctly answer a time-limited arithmetical skill-testing question. Value of prizes are in U.S. currency.

Winners will be obligated to sign and return an Affidavit of Eligibility within 30 days of notification. In the event of noncompliance within this time period, prize may not be awarded. If any prize or prize notification is returned as undeliverable, that prize will not be awarded. By acceptance of a prize, winner consents to use of his/her name, photograph or other likeness for purposes of advertising, trade and promotion on behalf of Harlequin Enterprises, Ltd., without further compensation, unless prohibited by law.

For the names of prizewinners (available after 12/31/95), send a self-addressed, stamped envelope to: Prize Surprise Sweepstakes 3448 Winners, P.O. Box 4200, Blair, NE 68009.

RPZ KAL